Dinner with Osama

the richard sullivan prize in short fiction

Editors
William O'Rourke and Valerie Sayers

MARILYN KRYSL

DINNER WITH OSAMA

University of Notre Dame Press

Notre Dame, Indiana

Published by the University of Notre Dame Press
Notre Dame, Indiana 46556
www.undpress.nd.edu
All Rights Reserved

Manufactured in the United States of America

Library of Congress Cataloging-in-Publication Data

Krysl, Marilyn, 1942–
Dinner with Osama / by Marilyn Krysl.
p.   cm. — (Richard Sullivan prize in short fiction)
ISBN-13: 978-0-268-03318-7 (pbk. : alk. paper)
ISBN-10: 0-268-03318-8 (pbk. : alk. paper)
I. Title.
PS3561.R88D56   2008
813'.54—dc22

                                    2007050580

♻ This book is printed on recycled paper.

FOR MY SUDANESE FRIENDS—

may they find peace and justice here in this country, and in Sudan.

CONTENTS

PART III

ACKNOWLEDGMENTS

The following stories have been previously published in slightly different form:

— "Dinner with Osama" won *Nimrod*'s Geraldine McLoud Commendation for Fiction.

— "Cherry Garcia, Pistachio Cream" won *Prairie Schooner*'s Lawrence Foundation Award for fiction.

— "Belly" appeared in *Notre Dame Review*.

— "Heraclitus, Help Me" appeared in *American Literary Review*.

— "Mitosis" appeared in *Washington Square*.

— "Air, A Romance" appeared as a letterpress chapbook produced by Tree Bernstein.

— Parts of "Welcome to the Torture Center, Love" appeared in *Fugue*.

I am grateful to the McDowell Colony, where I wrote "Welcome to the Torture Center, Love"; to the University of Colorado, which covered travel to the Brookings Institution; to the honor-able Francis Deng, whom I consulted in researching Sudanese history; to Peter Michelson, who contributed sagacious advice on the "Dinner with Osama" story; and to Julene Bair, Elisabeth Hyde, Lisa Jones, and Gail Storey, who offered smart, crucial commentary.

DINNER WITH OSAMA

I

Dinner with Osama

I'm on the Boulder mall half an hour before my herbal wrap appointment, shopping for an eyeliner not tested on rabbits, when I get the idea: Why not ask Bin Laden over for a glass of Chardonnay and something light but upscale? Me, Sheila, your average liberal neocolonial with a whiff of Cherokee thrown in way back when. I've been known to cook up a delicate Pesto Primavera or some boisterous Buffalo Enchiladas, take your pick. Better yet, something showy to appeal to his self-image as a major player—my Alaskan Salmon à la Tetsuya marinated in fresh basil, coriander, thyme, and grape seed oil.

Shoppers bustle past with gleaming, logoed bags. Though Osama's hosts, the Taliban, are anti-woman, I'm no threat. Think a latter-day Julia Child stuffing a Thanksgiving turkey. I've got a PhD in minding the human 7-11, serving all comers and keeping an eye on the clumsy bruiser who's about to knock the bottle of olive oil off the shelf. I'm an expert at chatting people up, and this is Boulder, where we aspire to getting it right. A passing tee reads, "meat: that's what's rotting in your colon." There's an ordinance against marketing fur within the county, and our Eddie Bauer carries the de rigueur parka with the built-in air pollution level monitor. Our city's joined the suit against global warming, and some of us have deeded our upgraded designer homes through trusts to the descendants of the original Arapahos. Shops specialize in North Korean ginseng, South Korean ginseng, Nicaraguan ginseng, and a fabulous new strain grown in Connecticut. You can order arias sung for the spleen tailored to your personal astro printout and, if the acupuncturist recommends it, get a liver massage.

The personal, my sis says, is perfectible. Limit kids' TV ration; then nurture away at the generous impulse. Sis and I are a year apart. I got the buxom look; she got svelte. We're like Do/ Don't, Before/After. She and Darin's dad couldn't get pregnant— they'd resigned themselves to our sperm bank, Immaculate Conceptions—and then they tried Gonal-F ampules made from crushed Chinese hamster ovaries, and this worked.

Sis and I were equal opportunity employers of unisex toddlers, and Sis's Darin had the nonviolent instinct from the start. He replanted stranded earthworms and got a sandbox rep for being the guy who gives away toys. In high school he got the male stride down but declined the Pall Mall swagger. Later he got into Chomsky et al and announced that he was majoring in International Meditation. It's all about fear, Darin said. You have to peel it away layer by layer. Wherever he is now, Darin would back my idea of wining and dining Bin Laden. Breaking bread with the enemy was Darin's rock and roll.

Darin was paying the rent by temping in the Towers when the planes hit. Sis and I rushed east, and talk about sobbing. We worked the streets with Darin's photo. This was the kid who kept shouting, Auntie! Look what I found! It's for you! Plump little hand thrusting out the latest-issue crimson leaf.

Grief is expensive—you pay right down to empty. You're a wrecked hulk, waiting to sink—but you don't sink. There came the moment when we had to get it: time to give up with the photo. We flew back on Prozac. Sis unlocked her place, went straight to the cupboard, and hurled every piece of wedding crystal against the parquet. She slashed the leather couch and matching armchairs with the cleaver, then flung her Dolce & Gabbana wardrobe into the grill pit, sprayed the pile with lighter fluid, and lit it. If I hadn't already shamed her out of her mink with my "fur is murder" tee, she'd have tossed the coat into the flames.

I wept and swept up. Then we bent our elbows and downed straight shots of Absolut.

—Remember that mother whose son got lynched in Alabama? Sis said. —After the sentencing, the guy says, Can you forgive me? And the mom says, I already have.

—I'm not there yet, I said. —Neither are you.

We kept at the Absolut. A few days later, when we looked up, all over the country the ancient revenge vibe was going strong.

—Revenge is dated, I said. —Who wants yesterday's flak jacket? Any way you cut it, retaliation takes its toll. Afterward you need a cruise, a laser peel. Finally, what have you got? A pound of dead flesh. What will you do? Bronze it?

—Darin, Sis said, came out against revenge before he could walk. He would not want a war declared in his honor.

Thus our letter to the president and Congress, our ad in the *Times*. Even as a kid, Sis wrote, my son refused to play with guns. Don't kill any Taliban boys for him.

After Darin went down, I fantasized buying a gun. The fantasy lasted ten seconds. Think Mother Teresa aiming an Uzi. When my kids flew the nest, I sold the SUVs and the Lexus, and got a condo and a mantra. Now I whip out compassion like it's an M16, and in my downtime volunteer with the county's Prairie Dog Low Income Housing Project. I've counseled the Bin Laden types, and I can tell you—Darin was right, it's about fear.

I know boys, and boys are not just a hot soup of testosterone. They act tough, while inside they're hovering over a powder puff. Take Darin's smile on first prom night. June doing its blossomy best to produce a seductive dusk, and I'm at Sis's place. Down comes Darin—black pants, white jacket—thrilled and scared.

—Hey, I said. —Look who's here: Drop Dead Handsome.

Darin's shy smile, like he's somebody's Christmas present.

You saw the photo of the Bin Ladens in the papers? The family in Sweden on holiday, gathered at the curb for the group shot. Osama's fourteen, bell bottoms and a Beatles cut, his most fervent wish to ride behind his brother on the moped. I recognize the ambience: he was shy around girls in fifth grade but hustled up daring and presented Shumailia with a Valentine box of chocolates. Osama was the pure flame burning and the petro dollars to make dreams come true. Then he got a little too ardent, this confused billionaire with a fundamentalist chip on his shoulder. Now he gets shunted from country to country attached to the dialysis machine courtesy of the American hospital in Dubai. Without it he'd be dead now, and damn if it didn't come from the Great Satan America!

And there are fashion implications: who can look chic on dialysis?

I get the word out to Abdullah, my pal at the gyros stand, that there's this invitation. Though I'm just a tad anxious about the atmosphere in my complex. I live above the Oaxacan muralist. Oaxaca is our Sister City. When Council banned smoking inside the city limits, they had a problem. What to do with fifty thousand gold cigarette lighters emblazoned with our mascot, the Peruvian llama? We gave Oaxaca the lighters; they gave us the muralist. My condo is over his.

Below and across from him the Palestinians moved in, and things were mellow yellow. Rehima lolled on the stoop in her scarf all perky smiles, and the aroma of tasty cookery rose to my level. Mohammed did math homework, Mehreen and the smaller kids chattered away, and when three-year-old Shafia cried, Mehreen took Shafia on her lap and the sobs turned into hiccups. Then an Israeli moved in across from me and above Rehima. No way around it: the presence of someone over you is cause for concern—what if there's a failure of trickle-down theory? Rachel's a sweetheart, but formidable with the magenta hair and spiked jacket over shimmering décolletage. And she turns up the volume and forgets to take off her boots.

Next morning she rushes down on her way to work at Cut Loose. Rehima stands in the doorway.

—You have murdered my children's sleep with your stomping of Sharon's boots!

Rachel rises on spiked heels and smolders past.

This morning when Rachel starts down, Rehima hurls a rock up to the landing.

—Why my children must study Hebrew! Why your schools forbid reading of great Palestinian poet Darwish!

Ours is not a complex where you invite guests without forewarning that they'll need an army pass and a friend in the Intifada.

Thursday morning my knocker bangs. I open. Abdullah's in Sufi ecstasy.

—*The fragrance that floats toward you at this moment,* he says, *streams from the tent of the secrets of God!*

—Osama says yes? I ask.

—Allah willing, Abdullah says. —Tomorrow at seven.

—What was it that convinced him? I say.

Abdullah turns up his hands. Allah is inscrutable.

I put on Madonna's *Erotica,* forward to Peggy Lee's "Fever," and clean the dining room. Next morning I buy the salmon, a dusky Chardonnay, and some Absolut, just in case. Then I stop at our third-wave feminist bookstore Word Is Out and pick up my special order of a gilded copy of the Koran.

—Hey, you with the clitoridectomy! Rachel shouts from the landing. —Where's your *jallabiya* husband? At the mosque with his rear end in the air?

Rehima hurls another rock up the stairs. —Have *you* crawled past sniper to get to water truck?! Have *you* given birth to sixth child while standing at army checkpoint?!

At six I shower and slip into full-length flax. Understated, and nonthreatening. Abdullah fills me in by cell phone. Turns out Osama couldn't finesse the border crossing in his private jet, so he stowed away on a camel shuttling heroin. In Islamabad he shaved. In Paris he got the Caesar cut with spiked bangs, the black leather jacket, Armani shirt. At Dulles, Security confiscated his fingernail file, but hey, here's a state-of-the-art dialysis machine, and Osama was cool, jacket dangling from a finger over his shoulder.

Abdullah drops him off and drives away. Think who you're hosting, I remind myself. Don't forget Darin's leaf—and remember, before the Towers there were all those dead Kenyans.

Rehima and kids mass on the porch. Osama pushes the dialysis machine up the sidewalk.

—*Shalom aleichem*, Osama says. —God is great.

—And there is only one, Rehima says. Eyes color of olive trees, cast down.

The kids surround him, chattering and bouncing. He passes out Milky Ways he bought at the airport. Mohammed holds out his math book and a pen.

—Can I have your autograph?

Osama signs, then climbs the stairs. I watch through the peephole. Between the spaghetti-strap top and hip slingers, Rachel's gold navel ring gleams.

—Tell me please, Osama says. —Where is your Sheila?

I open my door. —Osama! I say.

Rachel looks like she's just swallowed a matzo ball whole.

Osama settles into the wingback beside the window, where he can see the street. Dialysis machine like a bloodhound at his feet. He takes the Koran off the coffee table.

—Nice place you've got, Shelia. —And no mud. Afghan mud is satanic.

—Ordinance against mud, I say. —City council won't allow it.

He wants Absolut on the rocks, which I take as a hopeful sign.

—Sheila, he says. —Can we speak frankly? Think you could talk George into inviting me to the ranch like he does to Putin?

—But the Towers, I say.

—That was my groupies. Who can control them? They're convinced that Nostradamus wrote those Towers into the job description.

—George didn't bomb Mecca and Medina, I say.

—He will, Osama says. —Anyway my fans did George a favor. Your couch potatoes are waving his flag and investing in high-tech weaponry. He's got the next election in the bag.

I bring on the Portobello starter. Break a little bread together, I think, and armor clatters onto the parquet.

—Say I swing an invite, I say. —Think you could backpedal on the Satan thing?

—Sheila, consider. Jihad is a testosterone high. I'm Islam's version of The Rock. The *mojahedin* want my autograph. They want a photo op. And George took every video game I had! Half those toys are mine—more than half. And he stole your election!

Time for Fennel Salad with Lemon Zest.

—Have you noticed George doesn't have any pals? I say. Tony's just a wannabe. Legos are all George's got. If you called off the jihad, you wouldn't be backing down. You'd be stepping forward in a statesmanlike manner. Rising above petty petulance, demonstrating a hefty bit of tolerance and your own offshore savoir faire.

He likes the image. A little more Absolut and he could really get into it. Then he remembers the other image—he's been wronged!

—Sheila, he says. —There is such a thing as sharesies. Why aren't you sitting Georgie boy down and telling *him* to love the neighbors!? Osama's jaw tightens. —Clinton took in all those Sudanese boys. Let's see George take the Iraqi kids with heads that won't stop growing.

I think of Darin, the pudgy hand pushing that leaf. Beneath Osama's Armani there's a five-year-old with mud on his hands and an aching heart. I bring on the Salmon à la Tetsuya topped with chives and kombu on a bed of rice paper noodles surrounded by parsley oil and ocean trout caviar.

—Osama, what's the bottom line here?

He looks at me, eyes liquid anguish. —Let George be the one who's left out! Let him feel what it's like to be kicked around.

—It's not fair, I say. —Not fair. But remember: *Gold becomes constantly more beautiful from the blows the jeweler inflicts on it.*

—You Sufis, he says. But gently, like it's a compliment. Then he clears his throat. —The thing is, we've got the oil, and I've got a rep.

I sprinkle Chardonnay into his glass. —Say you call off the jihad and invite George to the table. You'll seize upper ground *and* up the quality of your rep. George will have to ante up, and you'll get the Nobel. Or you two can share it. What would it take?

—Tell George to get out of Saudi so we can get the king off our backs and worship without the metallic vibe of his fleet parked behind the mosque.

—That's it?

—And send Sharon to diversity training.

—And in return? I say.

—We call off jihad and send our women to college.

—What about the *mojahedin*? Some retraining's in order, don't you think? They need jobs, and you'd get points.

He considers. —Let the *mojahedin* take up nursing. Let them become art critics.

—Good thinking! I say. —So let's say you and George hit it off. There will still be all those little boys out there with guns. Let's find something else for them to do.

—Arafat solved it, Osama says. —When the Black September suicide bombers got out of hand, Arafat called patriotic young women to come forward and offer themselves to the nation. Marry the Black Septembers, he said, and we'll pay you two grand. Have a kid the first year, and we add five. Osama gives me thumbs up. —Give those boys with guns a girl and a check.

—The girls have to be free to say no, I say.

—Make the girls billionairesses, Osama says. —You can afford it. Direct deposit.

I bring the cappuccino chocolate mousse. We enjoy it slowly. A breeze wafts through the sycamore beside the open window.

—Help me with this Palestinian-Israeli thing, I say. —I don't think nubile young women and petro dollars will do it.

—Tough nut to crack, he says. —Maybe if you cook something for both.

—It will require many meals.

—But many meals are good. People make jokes. They plan trips to the sea.

—They fall in love, I say.

Much clearing of his throat. —This Rachel across the hall? Where is her husband?

—You want your kids learning Hebrew?

—Even so. Would roses be the way?

If Helen can launch a thousand ships, possibly Rachel can defuse a million M16s, G3s, Uzis, Kalashnikovs, and RPG-7s. I fantasize the offspring. Elihu and Harriet Bin Laden, Sumalia and Mohammed Weissman.

—Roses, I say. —And chocolate. And with the armor off.

Osama and I hear the sound at the same time. Abdullah's horn.

Osama stands. —Sheila, I owe you.

I flash on the dead Kenyans and pick up the Koran.

—Osama, you bankrolled some really bad produce. But that's behind you. So let's suppose one of your buttons gets pushed. Can you feel the forbearance kicking in?

He gives me a look that's absolutely level. —I push the buttons myself.

Darin's leaf floats up, his fat little hand.

—Osama, you said you owe me, and you do. My nephew went down with those Towers. Now I need you to abstain while I talk to George. When I've got him prepped, you and I will talk again. Give me that.

I lift his right hand, place it on the Koran. —Promise. No more towers until then.

He withdraws his hand. —See this dialysis machine? It cleans your blood. Once you start cleaning blood you can't stop. You have to marry the machine.

Oh these boys! The world's treasures! All that fervor for what is high and good—sharesies!—and what does Allah do? Sends renal failure.

—*Allahu akbar*, I say, groping for a way to pull him in.

—And there is only one, he says.

—Swear, I say. —For me. For your mother. For the planet.

At that moment my front door swings open. It's Rachel, thrusting out a CD.

—*Musiqah mizrahit*! she says. —For you.

—Forbidden, he says. He turns up his hands.

—Do not forbid yourself beauty! Rachel says. Her voice breathy, mint laden.

I withdraw discreetly. When I hear the dialysis machine descend, I go down. Rachel stands with Rehima, kids bouncing around them. Rehima smiles from her scarf and holds out a package wrapped in foil.

—Kabobs, she whispers.

Osama puts his hand over hers. —Keep them for Mohammed and the kids.

Osama exchanges a glance with Rachel: slow flames burning through the evening. Then he rolls the dialysis machine down the sidewalk. We watch Abdullah tool them away in dusk light. A turtledove coos in the sycamore. Rehima tells the kids to brush their teeth. Shafia starts to whimper.

—I want Milky Way!

Rachel picks her up. —Hey baby doll, she says. —It's gonna be OK.

I sprawl on the couch and bask. It went reasonably well. Now— what will I serve George? Roast Grouse with Bread Sauce? And on the side Braised Spinach and Daikon drizzled with parsley oil, garnished with leek. Pemican starter, a hearty Beaujolais, and for dessert? Apple pie à la mode.

I fall asleep on the couch. At three AM I wake to the shriek of sirens. Squad cars and fire trucks screech to the curb. Overlapping circles of light blare across our lawn. In the distance, rumble of things heavy and huge. Shiver of perception that this rumble is advancing. Think Waco without Reno: we used to call these monsters tanks. Now they're armored personnel carriers, and they're pointing at our building. I rush downstairs with Rachel. Rehima's door is open, and Shafia's crying. I go down the steps to the lawn.

Here comes the media, wattage and footage. Al Jazeera elbows out CNN. Reporters charge across the grass, and I'm unprepared—me. Here comes my fifteen minutes of fame, and what am I wearing? Couture flayed into submission. It gets worse. The reporters get me on camera, but in the blat of helicopter rotors they can't hear me. The helicopters hover, dropping commando soldiers. The commandos move so smoothly they must be on pills. They separate Rehima out like she's just another file card and strong-arm her to the curb. Rachel and I run to the rescue—though I get there first because I'm wearing Nikes from before the boycott.

—She's got eleven kids, I say.

—All she did was kabobs! Rachel says.

—She's pregnant, I say. —And she's not the one you want. I am.

A soldier steps in front of me. —Just go crochet some doilies, he says.

I take a deep breath and let it out slowly, the way Darin taught me. That remark was part of the young man's basic training. It's the trainers somebody needs to speak to, and I suppose that somebody will have to be me. But later. Everywhere I look there's every kind of rifle. It occurs to me to wonder what my file looks like. Did they note my check to the Department of Holistic Studies? My contribution to the Rapid Transit Deficit Bailout? My Kitty Dental Screening Fundraiser for the Humane Society?

Above and backlit, on a levitated platform resembling a cloud, Rumsfeld, George, and Billy Graham in Stetsons and alligator boots strut and frown. A fleet of swanky planes rattles the molecules of the air, getting into position to drop—what?

Fléchette shells? No. Down come the hardcover Bibles. Volumes thud down. They pile up. They dent the lawn. Abdullah forges through, touches my arm. His eyes soft, fragrant concern.

—Osama was afraid, Abdullah says. —He thought you'd turn him in. So he turned you in instead.

Darin said it: it's all about fear. Now George's voice blares through a Pentagon-logoed bullhorn.

—Come out now with your hands in the air!

—The kids! Rachel says. She grabs my hand, and we bolt through falling Bibles for the door. I hear a whack. Rachel makes a sound like a word she was about to utter has been jerked out of her. Her hand lets go, and she crumples on the steps.

—Don't forget Mohammed's dentist appointment! Rehima shouts. —And Mehreen needs help with math homework every night!

I grip the doorknob, but it won't turn. —Mohammed! I shout. —It's me, Sheila! I try to force the knob. Rehima's voice again, a spiral of ribbon falling from a package.

—And don't let Shafia run out into traffic!

Her voice is Darin's voice calling me across chilly autumn dusk, Darin running toward me with a handful of light. I want to tell Rehima she's not alone, I'll bail her out, they can't do this—not in my country! Just before the flash in which I see the bones in my hand, I turn like Lot's wife and look back.

Are We Dwelling
Deep Yet?

You want life—there has to be a death.

Call me Hathor, your author. *Is not my word like a fire and like a hammer that breaketh the rock in pieces?* Jeremiah plagiarized. I'm the original original—I brought forth myself myself. Now it's my job to keep the birthing going and oversee the unfathomable blossoming of fields where century after century grain sprouts, massive harvests pour in, and drunken harvesters dance amidst the spillage. Though this doesn't just happen. If you want lush produce, some guy has to die—but just one annually. With the help of our oracular Ravens I choose a consort, ravish him, cut his throat, let blood pour into the ground, and voilà—earth produces wheat, rice, frilly lettuce, snow peas.

That done, I must encourage maggots, sort rags of dead flesh. The job description spells out both aspects. It's a handful. I thought I'd slip into Boulder, Colorado, do the annual sacrifice, then take the rest of the day off, but no. Management institutes a speedup, and now I'm also supposed to settle things in the Mideast.

One minute I'm eternal and ethereal, then time to hang out in a fleshy body with greedy receptors and inquisitive longing—

and when that happens, the first thing I want is a latte. Plus seduction requires superior caffeine, which is why I'm treating myself to Vic's, across the street from Whole Foods, Prairie Dogs United, and the Palestinian Land Grant Fund. This time around I blend in as a coed in shorts, tank top, laptop, blonde hair long and straight as a horse's tail. Vic's impresario flutters glitter eyelids, whips up my latte like it's performance art, and I claim a sidewalk table and Google the *Times* front page: photo of Marines bursting into a Baghdad home.

Are Y'All Hiding Any Evil Ones In This Here Dwelling? The great grandmom age 103 sprawls in black robes on her back in terror, mouth open. Her grandson stands, hands up—Look Please See I Do Not Have Weapon! And oh please no—have Marines shot her great grandson? They HAVE, though they didn't mean to, but they were scared; who wouldn't be? This great grandson wasn't even married yet! *Must all young women become as widows?*

Marines mean well, but they track mud on Persian carpets. How whip those carpets back into glorious shape? Prez, do you hear me? The least you can do is pay the carpet-cleaning bill. All you have to do is tax the rich, just a little. Wave your flag, and tell them they'll be making A Living Wage possible for The Tired, The Poor, The Huddled Masses. They wouldn't want to be mere clanging cymbals, would they?

Say Oprah will want them on her show.

You have the clout to bring this off. Then you're free to tackle your legacy. Think upscale—something flashy and durable no one before you had the vision for. I mean the problem of evil, upper case, as in MOLOCH, that monster made of brass. *And they heated his lower parts, and his hands being stretched out and made hot, they put the child between his hands and it was burnt.*

You get the picture, Prez: sweet, dead kids.

But we only need one bleeding body annually. Granted, your trillion dollar overkill brings in bucks, but have you checked on the debits lately? The overkill, Prez, makes you look a little bit nervous. Seize the upper hand—do the smart thing, and astound your enemies: model greatness. Think of it: the cover of *Time*, *Newsweek*, you're right up there with Nelson Mandela. You can do it, because throw enough bucks at certain brands of Moloch, and it stuffs itself and goes off for a nap. Arafat gave the Black Septembers bucks to marry, have kids, and disappear, and it worked—they turned into potbellied CEOs.

This won't work with the Israelis, but you can fix that. Right now you give them five billion a year and say, Spend three bil buying our weapons. Then weapons must be used up by year's end—otherwise why make more? Olmert gives it hell, but is it easy using up that many Daisy Cutters so close to home? Not easy! Tell Olmert to use the three billion on demolition instead. Set the army's bulldozer drivers to demolishing the bulldozers, Uzis, and, yes, the wall. Imagine it, Prez: you're the one who brings the wall down. Shades of Berlin, jewel in your crown.

That done, your Nobel's in the bag. Cap it with Psalms: *behold, how good and how pleasant it is for brethren to dwell together in unity!*

Though with this unity thing, you'll need to set a solid gold bar example. Because after 9/11 you naturally went bananas, anyone might, but see my warning in Jeremiah 17:1: *Your unwise moves are written with a pen of iron and with the point of a diamond!* Think: Was it smart to rev up our red, white, and blue production lines and start turning out dead kids, ours and theirs? You've issued all ardent suicide bombers an invitation: come right in; Americans long to die!

April turns out sunshine like there's a surplus and we've got to use it up, and Boulderites are correct to a fault: witness Moe of Moe's Bagels pointing and urging his customers to go next door and patronize Tabouleh To Go. Boulder's perfect for the West's first suicide bomber. Why? We've got the money. We're dying to give it away, but philanthropy isn't easy. We tried giving it to Sister Cities, but we used up all there were. We tried funding Southern Sudan's Lost Boys and used them up too. Then we planned to bring all 34,520 Lost Girls to Boulder, but INS bureaucrats refused our bribes. Some tried flying abroad with bags of hundred dollar bills, but Security refused to let us board. The money just keeps staying here, so naturally those abroad feel slighted: Do *they* get to dine at Frasca?

No one would suspect a suicide bomber here because Council's declared Boulder a compassionate city. There's more meditation per square mile than in Lhasa and Varanasi combined. Stand at the corner of Fourteenth and Spruce on a quiet morning, and you will hear the communal in-breath and out-breath. And if it should happen that suddenly you feel especially cared for, know that seven thousand of your fellow citizens are doing Tong Len in unison. The *zabuton* and *zafu* markets are booming, Council's declared a monthly Poya Day every third Thursday, and all dental appointments, routine or otherwise, must be accompanied by massage.

Ninety-seven percent of Boulderites favor stem cell research, and those who don't are charged under Council's Negative Attitude Ordinance and sentenced to sixty hours of community service at the shelter, where our Compassionate City Ordinance mandates twenty-four-hour hot tub privileges and a martini of choice before the red pepper watercress filo parcels starter. Being a Compassionate City also led to Council's Nonslaughter of Mosquitoes policy. Council will import the appropriate mosquito predator once Boulder's Nobel scientists make a definitive determination, but in the meantime Council's Biosphere Balancing Ordinance requires the slathering on of DEET to prevent Council being sued by families of West Nile victims. This was a trade-off, but the good news is that Council hires sniffer dogs to detect non–DEET-wearing citizens, and this means jobs for our homeless residents training more sniffers.

Council strives to accommodate all comers, and should you object to DEET, you may apply for conscientious objector status. There is no challenge Council will not rise to, and lest anyone feel slighted and slump into inexplicable depression, our resident Tibetan monks pace the streets with their drums, calling citizens from seven figure torpor back to the glorious present.

What disguise would Boulder's bomber wear? See him with helmet astride the Waterford touring bike, bomb packs in each pannier? Or see her in Bloomingdale's full-length fur over the Ralph Lauren evening gown, bomb pack in the Gucci bag? Under Council's Emergency Assistance Ordinance anyone with a bomb pack could check into the Boulderado's presidential suite, receive the best pedicure in the nation with herbal wrap, then eat that last meal at L'Atelier. And would Bomber care for a final Rolfing session? Some last-minute life coaching? A glass of Chardonnay with the carrot mousse, the cumin zucchini and spinach ricotta shells, the Amaretto chocolate tart?

The mayor in running shorts sips espresso with Ram Dass, laptoppers update their Facebook portraits, and a redheaded mom perky with freckles parks a stroller two tables away and lifts out her boy kid. In cute camouflage shorts he trips after her into Vic's. It's a thrill, being in a body. Light looks shiny, molecules dither and swivel along my neural pathways, looking at passing hunks buzzes my pheromone receptors, a woman walks past twirling a sprig of lilac, little kids look excessively innocent, and the cuteness just doesn't stop. Mom and Cutie come out with her latte, and she situates him with juice and a power bar. She has that look: there is much world to attend to, and now this son. If another kid offers Cutie his toy Uzi, she'll let him play with it, but she's *not* going to buy him one.

Three squawking Ravens buzz over. Since Sumer, Ravens have had a rep for clairvoyance, but do we take advantage? We know how to plummet a smart bomb, flatten the property, and leave a hundred thousand wounded to die an agonizing death, but can we communicate with Ravens? You can help with this, Prez. Just tax the rich a teensy bit, and fund simultaneous translation and courses in Raven Speak. No Ravens left behind. And Boulder has bucks too—let's hurl some dollars at this now!

The Ravens circle low, and one squawks: look! FedEx drivers look drab in those uniforms, but this one steps smartly down looking like Michelangelo's David, though with skin from Bangalore. He's paying attention as though this is his first job—not counting retrieving baseballs hit over the fence, for which he got a dollar each. He carries a package into Moe's Bagels, and my pheromone meter flips to red. With all that black, curly hair and those biceps and thighs he could certainly plow my furrow.

He comes out, sees me. I keep the eye contact going—but he loses his nerve and lunges to the truck: back to work!

You're in a body, girl, I remind myself. Be more proactive. Caffeinate, and seize the day. The Ravens circle, checking out our air quality. We know how to make the world's best latte, but can we produce quality air? Every night the anchor makes the announcement: don't breathe if you don't have to. What we've got on this bright morning is more Moloch CO_2 clogging our air space. And do not tell me that the problem is that some breathe more than others. Everybody breathes equally—you too, Prez. This is a communal problem. Our worldwide communal vibe is at stake, Prez, and here on the front page lies this ancient Akka of a grandmother fallen on that muddy Persian carpet.

What's happened to our red, white, and blue respect for elders?

There she lies on muddy carpet, and here I am in the flesh, blissing out. Is this just? I'm forced to contemplate the Tree

Falling in the Forest Problem: If I'm not *there* where suffering *is*, does she feel my outrage at her pain? Of course not. She has no spare thoughts for me high on my latte.

If I were *there*, we'd be sobbing and lashing our upper bodies down like whips. I feel cut off from the life of mercy and friendliness. And meanwhile fishermen, who, granted, need to make a living, slice off sharks' fins for shark's fin soup, then toss finless sharks back into Great Mother Waters to bleed to death—and I'm spared!

I see where this is leading. It's leading to flying to Baghdad. If Akka Has To Breathe Depleted Uranium, I Should Have To Too. Though I don't want to go anywhere near depleted uranium, let alone breathe there. I sometimes want a few CEOs to breathe it a little, enough to get some human solidarity vibes going, but the minute I think about a single honcho coughing, I scream, No, I do not wish that.

So why am I not this minute where Akka is? Because when I'm in fleshy form, I'm your garden-variety coward. Reporters travel the globe and get beheaded, but not me. I mean well, but though I disapprove of polar bear extinction, I'm not going to the Arctic either. Why are there no smart bombs in the Caribbean? If there were suffering in Isla Mujeres, I'd go in a minute.

I whisper in Prez's ear. We could go *there* where Akka *is*, you, me, and Condi, on Air Force One. Are you up to drinking a mineral water with me? Getting chat going? Because I'm an inveterate chatter. I could chat even Condi into a corner. And unless you two opt for naps, I'll be saying some fairly obvious things. Like *Doth not wisdom cry at the gates and the coming in of the doors?* Are you aware that there's been no drinking water in Fallujah for months? Did you plan for a water convoy? I hope you did, because water is the least we can do, Prez. We who are becoming *brass and tin and iron and lead and are even the dross from the silver.*

Though do I want to get on Air Force One? If a suicide bomber's going to hijack a plane, that would be the one.

Cutie Pie toddles over and studies me. "You look really old," he says.

I lift him onto my lap and kiss his hair. "You're right! I'm really old." Only kids see my eons of Fertile Triangle mojo. Boulder's bomber had better spare Cutie, or Bomber will get zero virgins, nor will Bomber get another rebirth. I point up. "Look."

Cutie's amazed: Ravens! One peels off, swoops down, and lands on Vic's sidewalk—and that same FedEx David/Apollo drives up across the street. He strides into Boulder Valley Cosmetic and Reconstructive Surgery. I head out to cross, but a stretch limo pulls in front of me. I wait for all of it to pass—but it stops midway. I try to walk around this excessively long limo—it's like hiking the Pacific Crest trail. When I get to the end of it, my FedEx hunk has driven briskly on.

Out of the limo steps a biz suit looking like the World Bank's minister of finance. He strides into Vic's, emerges with cappuccino and a *Wall Street Journal*, and gives me the Notice How Smartzy Rich I Am smile. He has no idea I'm Isis suckling Horus. I'm sorry to say that overweening greed led him and his cronies to devise noxious substances and dump the stuff around our hallowed ground. World sanitation is not what it used to be, and that flirting with uranium 235 was also not a smart idea. We had Paradise once, but now thanks to suits snorting lines of rapaciousness, our products are sleazy, cheapness spreads like herpes, and we squander our sacred faculty imagination designing labs for sewing shut the eyes of cats.

Does *he* oversee the fecundity of animals roaming and birthing, insect populations increasing and quickly dying, the layered light of rainforests, oceans' colossal depths—in other words, the breathing, sprawling gods?! No, and I'm tired of smiling at trillionaires. Hathor 18:16: *I will make their possessions to crumble, and may their lives become like a perpetual hissing, and may they dwell in everlasting confusion!*

This suit could be Boulder's bomber. You've seen the ad for the Volkswagen Polo? Bomber climbs into the driver's seat, Hamas print scarf at his throat, and barrels up to his target café. Though the suit would deliver his explosive device in the limo timed to detonate after he'd walked briskly into the bank.

Another Raven lands in front of Vic's and tries to walk, lurching like a drunk. Does this look like natural old age in Ravens? I don't think so. I glance around for FedEx. But this isn't a Here's Your Man Get It On Raven—this is a sickened Raven, brought low. These creatures come down to us from Mesopotamia, people! They sat on my outstretched finger when I was Maat, Big Mom of Truth, Justice, and Mercy, giving the sacred tablets to earth's first honcho—to teach him that capital punishment is a no no bad idea, as is robbing the poor, setting little kids on fire, and confining chickens in cages. In other words a big NO to making women and children weep. Nor should men weep, but now men weep every day. Must we do Lamentations over?

Raven falls onto its side. *How is the crown fallen from our head!* Cutie and I start toward her, but an earnest young biker wearing a whooping crane tee intercedes, scoops up Raven, and makes a dash for Avian Emergency.

I am, as we say, shaken. This is not just any species. This is a species that can tell us the only really important fact we have, which is how it feels to be dead.

And how can I pull off a seduction with all this Moloch flying around in the air?! Prez, Osama, and you too, Tony, do you hear me? Get a life!

———

All right, Hathor, time to stop with the cowardice thing. I must, as we do in my profession, wing it to Baghdad—with the aid of ointment of hemlock, henbane, belladonna, mandrake, and a touch of aconite, which disturbs the heartbeat and produces flight. I sail off and touch down on the muddy carpet next to Akka. Zap, we bond: it's the woman thing, nerve ends tuned to recognize the other ones who do birthing, nursing, cooking, cleaning, and organizing potlucks so that enemies may break bread and tequila gimlets together, disband their armies, and take up a nonlethal sport.

"It's a fact," I tell Akka, "that rifles reproduce. They're like herpes bacteria. Lock two rifles in a room overnight, and next morning they're piled to the ceiling."

Akka has a face like I've Seen It All, So Give Us A Break and Evolve.

"Let's lock Prez and Osama in overnight," she says. "Those two need a time-out."

"A long time-out," I say. "Even better, how about a global time-out for everybody? Nobody works for one year, and we all meet for peace talks at the beach—all that eternal washing in and washing out will give the Moloch makers perspective."

"Food is key," Akka says. "Enemies must share many meals."

"What can we serve Olmert and Fatah/Hamas? If we serve *yakhne u roz*, Olmert takes us off his guest list. If we serve brisket and borscht, Fatah/Hamas stomps out."

"We need neutral food," Akka says, "but food is not neutral. This is turning into a hostess's nightmare. If it were just women, would there be this menu issue?"

"Can you imagine Cindy Sheehan sitting down with Martha Stewart?"

"We'll insist," Akka says. "Prez eats tabouleh, and Osama eats apple pie, and they have to look in each other's eyes and talk."

Laptoppers Google, imagining their finely tuned comfort will simply go on. It won't, but men aren't the problem. We need them to keep the birthing going, to appear with roses on Valentine's Day, and to surprise us with outbursts of tenderness that erase the lists of their shortcomings we'd started. It's Moloch that's the problem, and the Suit is just one version. The other versions are us: average human beings laden with character flaws and the wrong circumstances. Given wrong circumstances we'll do anything. Even without a gun pointing at our heads we go berserk. All it takes is a wrong circumstance and us, tweaked.

The Suit's right hand has work to do: suppress true nature of product and spruce up product's image, downsize and announce layoffs, displace persons, fauna, flora, and build that dam. But Suit means well. Imagine him in snorkel gear showing wife and kiddies fishy rainbows under water, getting the family drunk on delight. They're like the rest of us in juicy bodies imagining we're innocent. You too, Prez. Don't think you aren't subject to human unconsciousness in which the left hand doesn't know what the right is doing, or it knows but lets the right go ahead anyway.

It's the Suit's marketers who've declared Moloch high fashion, and here comes a blonde honey dressed like a suicide bomber knockoff. Her belt is set with fake grenades, and her backpack looks like the bomber's Saturday Night Special. She strides past Vic's toward the Society in Solidarity with Wild Mustangs and Burros in the Black Hills, and strides in as though she's witnessed grave injustices to burros and now will offer succor.

Though who could possibly be anti-burro? But we know: anyone will be anti-burro when wrong circumstances and high greed levels prevail. Take your average beekeeper, for instance. The research is in: bees in orchards will not return to hives where Keeper left his lethal Moloch cell phone. But Keeper doesn't know this. His bees abscond, and he believes he's cursed while

Bill Gates is not. He'd like to sock Gates, but Gates does not stroll orchards. Now a sweetie of a burro with golden brown eyes wanders past, and Keeper is suddenly fiercely anti-burro. If he had a cleaver, he'd cleave burro now. He grabs his pruning hook and charges, but I put a large rock in his path. He stumbles, falls, yells. Terrified, innocent burro canters off.

What Suit and the rest of us need is that Raven who sits on the emperor's shoulder and whispers, Your Excellency, don't forget: one day you're going to die.

Aung San Suu Kyi is still under house arrest, so it's up to Akka and me to rake the beach sand smooth for peace talks. Abdullah of the white robe waves his peace proposal at Olmert, Ahmadinejad poses for a photo op in diving gear with large harpoon, Chavez and Castro chat up Tamil Tigers, and Chiapas's Commandante Marcos writes a poem. Akka and I put on our bikinis. She takes the mike.

"Heads of State, take note," she says. "See those Ravens swooping down on the strand and fraternizing happily with gulls?! Let these birds be our models."

The crowd cheers, and Akka signals the band for a drum roll. Enter Prez in jacket and tie, Osama in *jallabiya* with dialysis machine.

"We're at the beach," Akka says. "Where are your Speedos?"

Prez refuses to take off his shirt because of the prompter. Is this codependence, or what? Nor will Osama disrobe. Has he got a prompter too?

"Dancing's required for all," Akka says. "Osama, do you know how to salsa?"

Osama spreads his prayer towel. "Dancing's forbidden," he says. "But I will eat."

"If it's soufflé," Prez says, "I'm out of here."

Are we hearing this? This is sandbox rhetoric.

"Prez," Akka says, "you're not leaving. You either, Osama."

They speak in unison. "Why not?"

Akka and I trade looks: she and I take charge, and these two sign a peace treaty?

"Because in the beginning," Akka says, "Hathor and I were there!"

Will I ever get to take the vacation days I've accumulated?

"Have you two balanced on a box blindfolded while Eminem raps? Birthed sixteen kids whose heads won't stop growing? *Forsake not the law of thy mother!*"

Where's Marshall Rosenberg when we need him? Akka and I will have to give the conflict resolution workshop ourselves.

"Take a deep breath, Prez," Akka says, "and let it out slowly. Osama, you too. No more lattes until you stop with the cowboy insurgent bit."

A Raven lights on Prez's shoulder. "Hathor 49:8," Raven says. "*Flee ye, turn back, dwell deep.*"

Wouldn't you know it's Ravens who go bilingual? Prez has that blank look he had when the 9/11 news came.

"What the Raven means," I say, "is *flee ye* from assisting Moloch."

Akka speaks into the mike. "Are we dwelling deep yet?"

The crowd is silent.

"Learn from the Bonobo," Akka says. "They do sex *instead of* aggression. Say there's a little guy stealing another kid's breakfast. A nearby female gives him a whack. Little guy's mom gets upset; after all, this is her baby. She confronts the female who did the whacking, and what happens? The two females feel each other up."

"And males hang face to face from a branch," I say, "rubbing erect penises together. How about the two of you give it a whirl?"

Osama kneels and bangs his head on the prayer towel.

Prez turns his back and folds his arms.

"This is going to be a long time-out," Akka says.

"I'll call the caterers and order more tabouleh," I say. "Then I want a swim and a margarita. You too, babe. Both of us need a chocolate truffle and a nap."

The mayor salutes Ram Dass, climbs on his bike, and pedals off. Suit tries to catch my eye, but I'm repositioning my hair behind my ears and keeping an eye out for FedEx. Cutie Pie examines a Luna bar wrapper on the sidewalk, and three more Ravens land wobbling: it's like whales beaching. I immensely don't like this. They flap into the parking lot, hobble a few feet, then flap up faltering, fly over Whole Foods, and disappear. I scan the sky. No more Ravens. Did we just witness the extinction of this superior species?

Suit eyes Cutie Pie's mom, but she's busy securing Cutie into his SUV of a stroller with a strap made to look like an ammo belt, each bullet flashing in neon. You can see her filling with bubbling protectiveness. She will throw herself in front of any barreling truck that threatens him. She will wrench the knife from the murderer's hand. And she will instruct him never to let a Marine recruiter sign him up. I close my laptop and follow them toward Whole Foods. Parking lot and bike racks are full. Noon rush spreads lazily in the sunshine. Cutie and mom go through Whole Foods' doors opening like the Great Vulva Vesica Piscis, which will then deliver them back into the world. The Great Harvest Bread truck, the Fresh Fish Fly-In truck, and the Fifty-Four Varieties of Olives truck park next to the Izze, Pellegrino, and Odwalla trucks, and FedEx Dionysus pulls up beside me and hops down with a package.

It's not just that I want one hand in those curls and the other squeezing his nifty rear. It's his eyes. He's seen things he'd rather not have, and so have mine, and he looks at me and knows I know.

I take hold of my side of the package: picnic basket with Beaujolais, two glasses? Inflatable mattress on which we'll reinvent sweetness? Package of stars beneath which he will tell me the key thing that has hurt him the most?

"Aphrodite," I say, with eyelashes. "Or call me Hathor; it's shorter."

"Osiris," he says, "or Shiva. Mom's Athens, Dad's Bangalore." His smile is slow, like hey, we've got time. "This is my last delivery. Give me five minutes?"

I watch him walk smartly through those doors with the package. Right then I decide: I'll find another sacrifice later—because I'm keeping this one.

I go around to the back of the store. The Ravens lie on their sides. Here and there breeze riffles a feather. I've seen species come and species go, but this time I lose it. I pop my aconite, wing it to the beach, land facing Prez. I remind myself that Prez too was once a Cutie. Barbara did her best, but Prez has forgotten that it's my yoni that makes it possible for people like him to eat steak and a baked potato, then *carpe* the *diem*.

"*Take the wine cup of this fury and cause yourself to drink it!*"

"Which one of you did this?" Akka says.

"Osama covets my Nobel!" Prez says.

Osama snickers. "You with a Nobel? I don't think so, dude!"

Akka's a weary Kali lowering the mike. "It was both of you together, wasn't it?"

That's when Jeremiah 25:31 hits Whole Foods: *A noise shall come even to the ends of the earth.* Ahmadinejad drops the harpoon. The sound of the blast rolls all the way out, then flattens into the sea's murmur. Abdullah's proposal falls from his hand, and wind scatters the pages. Commandante Marcos pauses in the act of writing the word *revolucíon*—or is it *revulsíon*? Down rain bits of steel girder, a gorgonzola, one shoe, part of a pineapple, a chunk of asphalt, one wild Pacific salmon fillet, glass shards. Half a loaf of Whole Foods' hurled hemp bread lands at Prez's feet.

Osama picks it up and offers it to Prez. "You like?"

You want life—there has to be a death. I imagine Cutie Pie's small face looking up: Mom?! And Osiris/Shiva unbuttoning the FedEx shirt, pulling the tee over his head, looking into my eyes— reaching for me.

II

CHERRY GARCIA,
PISTACHIO CREAM

A mother, a daughter, a beach. Sky, water. Gulls, mynas, also tiny canaries, bougainvillaea. Mild surf. The soothing, repetitive sound of its wash. Two women walk by, wearing swimsuits the mother thinks resemble flowered underwear.

"Those suits," the daughter says. "They look like they came from Kmart."

"Well, we don't."

"Absolutely not. We have class." The daughter laughs. Her declaration of solidarity follows on their decision to buy the same black bathing suits. The daughter tried on two-piece suits the mother thought ugly: daisy prints and those tropical floral numbers favored by grandmothers. The daughter didn't like them any more than the mother. I don't want to look like I'm still fifteen and confused, she'd said. She tried on the same suit her mother had decided on.

"You look smashing," the mother said.

In the daughter's mind her choice suddenly became clear. She and her mother were a pair, handsome women. Of course this was the suit she wanted. Its understated elegance described whom she'd finally become: a woman as worldly, poised, and competent as her mother.

Bathers coming in, other bathers going out. A short Japanese father walks past, followed by his tall son. The daughter is fascinated by this tandem rite. Her own father, who once commanded a large part of the foreground, now seems to stand somewhere behind her and her mother. Or not stand but recline, in a recliner, pipe beside the glass of bourbon and water, while he follows the progress of a documentary on the courtship practices of bowerbirds.

He'd had to forego this vacation in order to complete the design for the new Performing Arts Center, part of the general refurbishing of the state capitol. The mother and daughter were secretly pleased. They wouldn't for the world hurt his feelings, but right now they want to feel completely free to indulge mother-daughterness. They want to giggle together in a conspiratorial way, to be impetuous, even rash with their mutual affections. Though they know he would never object to this, that he would in fact take pleasure in their pleasure, still their solicitous regard for his feelings would cramp their style.

The Japanese father has the gait of a Sumo wrestler, out in front of his son, insistent on primacy. Or perhaps this son truly honors this father, who is beginning to need to lower his cholesterol. Though the daughter has the impression their tandem is less the son's choice than the result of centuries of custom, custom in which sons as well as daughters were obliged to assume the position of females. Such protocols are crumbling, she believes, and not a moment too soon. Though the Equal Rights Amendment failed, though women still make sixty-nine cents on the dollar—for a while it was seventy-nine cents, but it's gone · back down—we are living in a new world. And it belongs, here and now, to egalitarian mothers and affectionate daughters. Imagine walking behind your mother—preposterous!

"Are you coming in with me?" the daughter asks.

She takes her mother's hand, as though she wants to declare their love in public. The daughter's long hair is straight, an auburn waterfall. The mother thinks maybe she'll let her hair grow too. She smiles to think she's taking her daughter as a model. Also the mother does not tire of noticing how the daughter tosses her long hair to one side, how they share the same slenderness, the same voracious metabolism. They eat a lot and often, then burn it right up. Hand in hand they walk toward surf: a double set of Renoir brush strokes, moving toward water. They go in waist deep, stand there. The water is pale turquoise. Suddenly the daughter ducks down.

"Chilly!" she says. She kicks, putting a little distance between them. "Come on!"

The mother follows her. They paddle idly, not going anywhere, being in motion together.

Things are peachy keen, and I know what you're thinking. It's not a story unless something goes dramatically wrong. You want dissention: conflict, the frisson in each scene upping the ante, leading to catharsis. Catharsis is what Aristotle prescribed, and to get you there the characters have to suffer. Suffering is uppercase. No comic interlude should interfere with the smooth, ongoing flow of treachery. OK, all right, once in a while you'll accept a happy ending, but only after harrowing distress.

But think about it. These two have a major fracas? Not likely. They're into affectionate cooperation, gooey love. The daughter likes holding her mother's hand while they walk, and the mother eats this kind of thing up. The mother could dislike the daughter's boyfriend, but that's so predictable, and besides, he's a sweetie. He and the mother go for each other. She's beginning to indulge the notion that he's the son she didn't have. One of them might find out belatedly about a much earlier betrayal by the other. But betrayal is also predictable, and frankly I don't like it. Where Hippocrates says, *friendship is treacherous*, I like to quote him as saying, *experience is treacherous and friendship fleeting*.

Anyway, these two had their torment much earlier.

After the mother worship of childhood, the daughter, at twelve, at fourteen, at sixteen, had felt the mother's presence nearly unendurable. This mom ran marathons. She climbed Mount McKinley. She chaired the Department of Theater and Dance at the university and had played all the female leads in Tennessee Williams, and she'd got rave reviews for her Lady Macbeth, her Kate in *Taming of the Shrew*. She sat on the State Arts Council board and helped organized the annual AIDS Walkathon. There were many finish lines, and life whizzed by at high speed, a strong breeze snapping the mother's flags.

Or so the daughter told herself when she felt uncertain of her own capabilities. Actually the daughter was well aware that though the mother's competence seemed formidable, she needed wrapping and cuddling, little strokes and kisses, compliments and presents. Though the mother could hold her own in a marathon, she was easily wounded. Though she spoke to large crowds without anxiety, she could be stung by a cruel remark. The daughter wanted to hurt her, just a little. It felt good, sometimes, to turn coldly away.

The father had told her that once when he and the mother quarreled, he'd suggested that she dramatized things, perhaps overly. His wife looked at him and laughed.

"What you get is what you get."

To the father this remark seemed titillating. He'd laughed. But when the daughter listened to the story, she heard the mother's remark as a stiletto of ice. Soon after hearing this story, the daughter hurled a soapy dishrag at the mother and stomped out of the kitchen. How dare this mother feel so sure of herself!

Why couldn't she have a mother less spectacular? Someone who sometimes hesitated would have been nice. Someone a little less directed, softer, dreamier, less tightly knit.

"You always know what you want, and you get it," the daughter said. Her hair was matted on one side from lying on the bed, sobbing. "Why can't you once in a while not know?"

Gone the mother's élan. She became an ache. Hot baths didn't help. The word "until" presented itself in the air and stayed there, ringing like a phone no one was answering. She remembers that time, several years, as a hair shirt she could not take off. Every moment—and the present was eternal—she was cast out. She could not find a way back into the daughter's affections. The daffodils came forward, tulips spread their arms wide, but it was as though she stood outside her own house, locked out. No fluffy bed, no boiling tea kettle for her! No cozy hugs while she and the daughter lounged on the couch, watching a Nora Ephron movie. No shampoo and conditioner camaraderie, no girly solidarity against pipe smoke and football. No little presents in the fringed box the daughter made at the Third Grade Art Fair, where, beneath the clam shell lid, she left Magic Marker love notes and, on Mother's Day, a chocolate truffle.

The father watched from the sidelines. After the soapy dishrag episode, he'd slung an arm around his wife's shoulders. She'd wept. He'd embraced her, patted her back. She went on weeping. He'd had the good grace not to say, "This too shall pass."

Then the daughter called off her onslaught. Suddenly she seemed very busy. She left home, got educated, and took a job as therapist, counselor, and general troubleshooter at the Safe-House. The women who fled there were terrified, confused, indecisive women. Their vacillation was excruciating. They smoked one cigarette after another while they tried to make up their minds whether or not to leave the men who were hitting them and their children. In the course of ministering to these women, the daughter came to know herself more exactly. She was not, she noted, nearly so anxious, so tentative, so helpless as these women. In their presence she possessed a confident common sense and its attendant generosity, and a very large capacity to imagine their terror, their uncertainty, their longing. These qualities had been in her all along, but she had not fully experienced their dimensions until called upon to do so. In this context the nuance of her acts, which had seemed clouded by the shimmering figure of the mother, appeared in all their rich, palpable detail.

One day the mother dropped in unannounced. As she entered the hallway, she saw a band of coworkers swoop into the daughter's office, bearing armfuls of blossoms. It wasn't the daughter's birthday. So this daughter contained surprises! And there was the time she'd overheard the daughter speaking to her father like a counselor. "You might try," the mother heard her say. What were they discussing? It was the daughter's air of wise competence that caught the mother's attention. And when she goes to the daughter's apartment—for now the daughter has thrown open that locked door—there are new recipes simmering, the aroma of unfamiliar spices. All these things could happen without her, the mother! Amazing, she thought. My daughter has a life.

Now the daughter feels affectionate. What once resembled photo realism in the daughter's mind has taken on the character of a Mary Cassatt. When she was a child, she would carry a leaf or a pebble into the house to offer her mother. Now she has again begun to bring her mother little gifts—a coupon, a new kind of candy bar. Earrings. Choosing the same swimsuit is another version of these presents.

———

So you see: all that's over. Here they are at the shore, in love with each other. When you're in love, you refuse to let anything spoil it. And this is not your average chocolate chip cookie love. This is baked Alaska love, replete with nostalgia about little things that mother and daughter have now decided to render significant by dwelling on them.

Still, you say, we cannot let these two simply persist! Persistence is not a story unless it translates into triumph over overwhelming odds. Conflict is rising action in the realistic mode, bristling with interesting abrasions. It requires AK-47s and ammo. You're used to bloody crashes, exploding mines, death by drive-by shooting, the bombing of executive towers.

All right: for you, I'm prepared to invoke the conventions to which we've become accustomed. A young man changing a tire on the interstate gets offed by a passing motorist. Russian wives pay cash up front to have alcoholic husbands blown away. Shell trashes the Ogoni; the Mexicans trash the box turtles. Refugees trash each other for a cup of water. And fifteen-year-old Martha Moxley is beaten to death with a golf club on the grounds of her family's exclusive estate in Greenwich, Connecticut.

The mother and daughter sip mineral water beneath palms. They watch two vans pour out their stream of primary school children. The kids run, shouting, toward the pier. They run to the end, scream, and jump off, clutching their knees with their arms, hitting the water in fetal position. They fill the surf, bob, run up onto the sand.

These kids are mad exuberance. Unbounded energy. The mother and daughter are charmed by their running and shouting. When the daughter wearies of watching them, she likes to look at her mother's body. She can't tell if her mother is beautiful, or if she thinks so because this is her mother. She studies the little nicks—pimple, lizard skin elbow, a tiny bruise on one thigh.

"You've still got those great legs," the daughter says.

"I'm not too happy about my face though. It looks kind of saggy."

"So what if it's not the face of a twenty-five-year-old. That would be weird."

"Still," the mother says. She laughs. You can discuss your neurotic anxieties with a daughter, then giggle together. It's fun to have foibles to titter about. Two little girls in ponytails run to the end of the pier, take each other's hands, and jump off.

"Your grandmother really was good looking," the mother says. "And she gave us both these good bones."

The mothers call the children. One boy insists on running one last time onto the pier and jumping off. He scrambles out, runs to catch up. Children, the mother thinks, are ever seeing some brightness and rushing toward it, until they remember: Mother! Where is she? Then they tear back, flinging themselves at her with everything in them.

The daughter watches two mynas instruct their offspring in scavenging. Beyond them sea offers infinite slipperiness. Every evening the same sunset: clouds, pale gray, and behind this scrim, a hot pink ball. Night, when it comes, will be a nest. Birds roosting, palm fronds rustling. Soon they'll discuss what they want for dinner, whether the restaurant will offer key lime pie.

"Tell me everything you remember about me when I was little," the daughter says.

"When you started to talk, you chattered away nonstop. You kept up running commentary on everything you were doing. Now I'm putting Jane's shoes on—remember Jane, your first doll? Now I'm putting Jane to bed. Now I'm sitting down on the potty." The mother remembers how sweet the daughter's body had seemed, how she held her and kissed her and felt soft baby skin against her own. "And you used sophisticated words you'd heard people say. One day you watched a car drive by, and you said, 'What a delicate car.'"

"I didn't want you to have any children but me," the daughter says.

"Once you and I were driving somewhere, and you asked me if your father and I were going to have another baby. You were eight or nine, I think. And you declared yourself. You said, 'I want to be your only child.'"

"And you heard me," the daughter says.

"Of course," the mother says. "You were wonderful. How could we have wanted more?"

Extravagant assertions! But really, what delight, this trading of compliments, this basking in mutual trust. Springy, like the mesh of a hammock so wide you can't fall out of it.

You still don't like it. All this joie de vivre is not how people actually have to live their lives. There is no free lunch. This mother and daughter enjoy their glass of sparkling intimacy while another mother and daughter are made to watch each other being tortured. But of course: it happens. Our psyches have been battered; thus we require battering. Comfort us, you say, with the usual double on the rocks and an olive of titillation on a toothpick.

But what's true at one juncture of the space-time continuum is not necessarily true at another. And what's true, right here, right now, is that bliss reigns, interrupted by occasional trips to the toilet (an act not without its own pleasant slant on sensuality!), or into the café to get a latte. Notwithstanding the fact that in a London subway a bomb is exploding, that in the Balkans a dead man lies face down in a burst sack of flour, what's going on here is bliss, prettily punctuated by modestly lavish sunsets, and little children who shred our cynicism. Not one single kid is sobbing. There isn't even one skinned knee!

You protest. Don't distract us with a shiny bauble! We have to live in the real world, and it's hell out here. Listen, I hear you. Still, at every moment reality is up for grabs. You've constructed your reality, and your take is indeed savvy. But it's a construction. So is mine, of course. But right now I prefer mine, replete with sudden bursts of irrational well-being, affection that resembles an underground spring bursting up through the crusty earth. I'd like to talk you around, however briefly, to checking it out. Come on over: it's free and mellow yellow, here where there's no matricide, no child abuse. Here where the sand has been raked into evenness and the water is shamelessly gorgeous.

The sea, the mother thinks this morning, is a monster. They've scarcely finished breakfast, and already she's lost an earring in the water. At first she felt that a precious object—almost a part of her—had been stolen: her daughter gave her these earrings! But then it seemed fitting: of course you must give something up to this animal roiling! Great grandmother beast—bone washer, rock breaker, lady of the floating hair gobbling dead sailors. Primalness must have her sacrifice, the mother tells herself. Think of it as feeding the ancestor.

They settle into chairs. Before them, two lovers on the pier, woman in bikini, man in wetsuit. He has unzipped the wetsuit halfway and thrown off the top so that it hangs down his hips. The top of the woman's head comes to the middle of his breastbone. She is darker than he is, her long black hair in a braid. They hug. When he lets go, she grabs his arms, puts them around her.

"Jack used to do that," the daughter says, remembering another boyfriend. "He'd let go too soon, and I'd have to take hold of his arms and put them back around me."

"Some of them have a hard time reading signs," the mother says. "But your father wasn't like that."

"Neither is Alan," the daughter says. Her present boyfriend is a first-class cuddler. He seems to want to cuddle even more than she does, and without it necessarily leading to sex. He even has a word for it. Nuggies, he says. Let's have some nuggies. The daughter lies back in the blue cocoon of a towel. She reads a book, *Investing for Women*, but it's boring. She lets the wind turn some pages.

"It's nice to piddle around," the mother says. "I don't have to make a list of things to ask you because we only have an hour."

The daughter smiles. The mother remembers those years when she saw her daughter infrequently. When the time came for their lunch, she'd been too anxious to enjoy it. There would be scarcely enough time to talk about what was crucial, let alone important past and present trivia. And she needed more time just to look at her daughter! She missed drinking in that pertness, her daughter's freckled complexion that sunburned easily, and the furrow in the daughter's brow caused by serious consideration of things like the Palestinian-Israeli question.

The lovers come onto the sand. The man strips off his wetsuit. They towel themselves, and the woman asks him to oil her. He obliges and, when he finishes, kisses her shoulder. A few divers toting gear walk onto the pier. A boat approaches, docks. The divers climb on. The mynas have flown. The daughter's book lies open on her lap. Her eyes are closed.

Parents should die before children, the mother thinks. But this is often not the case. Children get cancer, or they're killed in war or run down by drunk drivers. The mother imagines how easily her daughter could be hit by a stray bullet from a gang fracas or from the gun of a crazy person going ballistic in a mall. Or she could die of something toxic, aluminum in deodorants, acid rain or arsenic. Or something not yet detected, say a substance used in the manufacture of rayon. She imagines the daughter, ignorant of this, buying a poison dress that will kill her in five years.

Cherry Garcia, Pistachio Cream 45

The daughter wakes, takes a drink of water. "We could eat something," she says.

"Wait just a minute," the mother says. She stands up with resolve, strides to the water, wades out up to her waist. Takes off the other earring and drops it in. *Take this, Old Gal, and be full. If it isn't enough, tell me. Tell me if I should give up my Subaru, start tithing. As for me, I have only one request: pass, please, on the live sacrifices. Or if you have to have them, please, not daughters.*

So: I've introduced a flutter of dread. Are you happy now? This is only a fear, of course, and inevitable. Mothers by definition must anticipate the worst. Hence all those St. Christopher medals, those admonitions not to talk to strangers. But you like the fact that I've invoked uneasiness. You perk up. Ocean, you think, is the obvious unpredictable element. Even I can't command it. Let's hear it for water's ubiquitous egalitarianism, which it pulls off by subsuming everyone and everything. Ocean does not discriminate between diamond ring and rubber band. Pretty thisses, precious thats are the same in its maw.

Say the daughter swims out too far. In the space of one human breath, the sky can shift a shade darker, and the molecules of air above the water begin to quiver. The daughter might dawdle in sensual rebuttal, not thinking of anything at all, feeling her body laved in this clean brine. Then—suddenly—the water around her is roiling. It's raining. A smashing wind blows her bobbing body further out. Though she paddles with everything she's got, the shore recedes. The mother marshals the hotel's staff—

But it isn't even the rainy season! There are not going to be storms here, not now. Of course the daughter could die in a storm sometime in the future. But it isn't going to happen today, or to-morrow, or the day after. There could be sharks—but there aren't, only a few baby barracudas. The daughter could have a heart attack while floating in this liquid nest—but no. This young woman's heart is a Gold Medal muscle.

What we've got is sunny and mild, and now they're going to stroll toward the restaurant. OK, all right. I know. So just for you, because I like you, here's one last pan of conflict quickies. Man depositing small child in wooden box, closing the lid, hammering the lid shut. The orphanage in Menoufiya, torched to destroy evidence of selling children's body parts for transplant. Those cremations in which the widow gets to climb on top of her man and go along. And in the distance the Indonesian rainforest crackling, smoky haze drifting over the sea.

Or I can get you seats even further back, add a scrim of irony. Think London, the bananas flambé served by Pakistani waiters to the heads of this year's ten most successful corporate polluters.

What happens is tortilla soup, a nap. When they wake, it's back to the beach, towels and books, sunscreen and lemonade. Mothers with babies arrive. The tots who can walk sport water wings. The smaller ones are placed on the water in inflated devices resembling small boats or huge ducks. Lemon yellow and fuchsia bathing suits are big. There is floating and digging in the sand with plastic shovels. A boy brings his sister a shell. A girl carries a handful of sand to her mother. And two brave three-year-olds make a pact, fall backward together into the water.

The mother remembers how the daughter brought her caterpillars, leaves, how she laid these treasures at her mother's feet. How the mother leaned over, admiring each item, examining the daughter's precious head, the little hands. So much longing to be good, so much giving and receiving. Isn't it something, how this goes on.

"I used to kiss your feet when you were a baby," the mother says. "You had the sweetest toes, and your knees were fat." The daughter laughs. "And the day you sat down with pencil and paper, wearing a pair of underpants on your head. Was it fifth grade? When I asked, you said the panties were your thinking cap, which you needed to win the Daughters of the American Revolution's historical essay prize."

"Oh Mom," the daughter says. She smiles. She remembers the years of being angry at her adolescent clumsiness, afraid of not knowing the things she'd needed to know. Now if one of her women is afraid, she locks the Safe-House door and phones the police department for her.

Two boys arrive with their father. There is much maneuvering of buckets and shovels. The father assists the excavations, the construction of a moat around a castle. When it's complete, the smaller boy wants to be buried. While late afternoon clouds prepare another sunset, his father and brother oblige him.

"Let's swim out," the mother says. "The sun will soon be down."

They stroll into surf, strike out for deep water. Side by side they crawl, breaststroke, sidestroke. When they're sated, they float on their backs. The mother looks up at clouds, their shapes shifting, in drift. She remembers a night when she and two other women were on their way to a concert. They'd had to park far from the hall, cross a soccer field, or was it three soccer fields? The space they'd had to traverse seemed vast, and they were wearing long coats and high heels.

"Let's run," the mother had suggested. Side by side in their flapping coats, their ridiculous shoes, they ran, laughing and panting, and as they ran, they filled with an energy that resembled elixir. Though this was just the by-product of exertion, it came as an unexpected charge.

For the most part, she thinks, her life has been like that exhilarating running across a field. It's about energy, she thinks.

Or the coming and going of energy, the lapping back and forth of those waves. Now you see it; now you don't. Now you see it again. Which energies will sweep to the fore, take us beyond our smallness? She does an inventory. She has made large gestures, yes, but has she become a larger person? What exactly would a larger person be?

But why this self-interrogation? They came here to bask, to bathe, to sleep. She doesn't have to think about improving her character. She doesn't even have to take stock. No one's counting. She looks up at cirrus drifting above her. Feels the lavish water.

The daughter giggles. "I feel like some fisherman's bobber," she says.

The sun is low, just a little above the horizon.

"I wonder if you could fall asleep here, being rocked like this," the mother says.

"And if you did, would you keep floating?"

"Fish sleep, don't they?"

The daughter giggles again. "Do we know that for a fact?"

They're pretty far out, aren't they.

You anticipate the swell coming out of nowhere, suddenly engulfing the daughter, and also the mother! Both, in their softness, in their hurtable bodies, into the teeth of this devourer! Maybe one of them makes it, maybe neither, you think. It's got to be one of those two.

But I'm telling you, notwithstanding the towering past, it doesn't always happen that way. The sea stays calm. Their hearts don't miss a beat. The air keeps pumping these two with just the right amount of glorious oxygen. The water at its amniotic best, rocking their bodies, lapping them with its lustrum.

Believe me, the honor killings and the drafting of children into military service will continue without your anxious anticipation. But now we're here, and here it's Take Your Daughter to the Beach Day. It's the Week of Painted Toenails. Girls' Month. The Year of the Yoni. Nipples are in, and so are midriffs, navels. Slit skirts and skirts mid-thigh are going strong, and the stock of mother-daughter liaisons is up. Joyful teasing and dainty carousing are in.

So it's not your reality? But it could be!

Or think of it this way. I'm serving Pistachio Cream, and you want Cherry Garcia. But has it occurred to you that a time will come, sooner or later, when there won't be either? OK, you still want Cherry Garcia. What can I say? Either way, it's *carpe diem. Carpe diem*, friends, is all we've got—until we don't.

They walk out of the surf, panting, buoyant. Behind them the sun floats in that rosy zone just above the horizon. The daughter shakes water from her hair. How good a thick towel feels, the pleasant roughness just after you've exerted yourself. The Japanese father and son stroll past in their customary tandem. They remind her of a small Japanese girl she saw once in an airport lounge. The little girl was maybe three, not more. She'd turned to her brother, taken his hand, and tugged him forward until they were running. On her face an expression of utter happiness. She was leading them both toward some lit, shining adventure. Perhaps this was simply the adventure of running across a very large room, but they threw themselves into its ecstasy. It's the kind of joy the daughter feels now with her mother. As though they run hand in hand toward some dazzling.

"We're living happily ever after, you and I," she says, smiling at her mother, as though this state of affairs is their doing, a joint project.

But the mother frowns. "You know how I detest even coming down with a cold. It's going to be hell when my body really starts to fail."

The daughter stops combing out her hair. "That's not going to happen for years, Mom. Anyway, when it does, I'll take care of you."

It's a sentence like one of those leaves or pebbles the daughter, at two, brought her. Now the mother tries to imagine herself crippled, in a diaper, catheter and other tubes out the wazoo, unable to sit up by herself, needing someone to feed her, unable to hear much, seeing dimly.

"You'll haul my bag of bones out of bed—is that it, sweetheart?" She is trying for jauntiness. "Pop me into my wheelchair?"

"Exactly. I'll push you to the top of the hill behind your house, tool you around in the sunshine. All you'll have to do is absorb the vitamin D." They laugh. I'll this; I'll that. It's the kind of thing the daughter used to say when she played doctor and came to bandage the mother's arm. The daughter's hair smells of sea brine. Her skin is smooth as the inside of an abalone shell. "There you'll be," the daughter says, "me beside you while you tell the politicians to go to hell." The daughter flexes her elbow and pulls up her biceps the way the body builders do it. "We can't be stopped!" the daughter says.

Me teetering on the edge, the mother thinks, and she'll be waving the flag of Forever!

Not that the daughter is in denial. She simply wants to reassure the mother, to foreground their love. And to invoke the flex of their power. We can't be stopped. The mother herself has indulged this attitude on numerous occasions. It's an illusion, of course, but *très familier*. You feel in these irrational moments not only that you can handle whatever comes up, but also that you're probably immortal. At least you're going to feel immortal for most of the rest of your great swatch of time. So hey, take more! Don't stint! There's an endless supply!

Suddenly the mother gets it: the other earring won't be nearly enough. Had she really imagined the maw would be sated with a couple of clinking trinkets? *Let me be the first to go*: a common enough wish, invoked in the attempt to protect one's child from harm. But that was really a way of creating the illusion that you have a say in this matter of mortality. Let me at least decide the sequence here! Then—a little touch of Hollywood—you imagine yourself brave, stepping forward, into the watery mouth.

The sun quivers on the surface of the horizon and, where it begins to touch the water, sends out lengths of shimmer. The mother remembers a day when she was forty, the daughter sixteen. All afternoon leaves had been falling, lazily, one by one. Her life felt peachy keen. There were no holes in it. Though now the daughter was occasionally difficult, this was due to the confusing, contradictory cocktail of adolescence spiking her juices. This stage would pass. The daughter would learn to fly, and their rapport become a place of birdy soaring.

The daughter had come home from school then. She'd walked in the door, walked past her mother in the dining room, and not looked at her, not said one word. She'd gone to her room and slammed the door. A bad day, the mother had thought. Some incident in the locker door–slamming halls of the high school. She knew she shouldn't take it personally. But it had felt like one of those deaths where they don't find the body. In that moment she understood she loved her daughter more than she loved her husband, her parents. Not differently. More. She'd kept this to herself, because she hadn't wanted anyone to feel slighted. She hadn't even told the daughter—what if such love seemed ungenerously narrow? A person ought to love broadly, profligately. She didn't want the daughter to think she was a clinging, niggardly person.

She'd taken her love out then and looked at it. She loved her daughter with a shameless, greedy, exclusive love. *This one and no other.* No one should love that way. It wasn't balanced. It wasn't moderate. It had been the reason she hadn't wanted another child.

No one should love that way, but she had.

Does.

Half the sun has sunk. Afternoon, giving itself to dusk. The daughter combs her hair, humming, working on a tangle. Over the daughter's shoulder the mother sees the Japanese son walking down to the water alone. Where's the father? Reading the *Tokyo Times*? Taking his blood pressure? She watches the son dive in. There he goes, kicking away from the coast, going after the light as though he thinks he's got a shot at it.

BELLY

Operatic Belly

Charlie Rose should interview me on the subject of the belly. I'd sing the belly's praise like the soprano I am. How it smolders! How it revels in this smoldering. I'd arpeggio how it's the Marilyn Monroe of the body. How Chopin anticipated it and Debussy referred to it elliptically. How it makes the stock market shoot up and the Nasdaq flourish. How its extravagance troubles the pope.

How it advances even as it is stationary.

I tra la la for a living. See me standing in the arc of the chorus, lilies in a bed opening our throats. We sing of love and betrayal, jealousy and sorrow. Fury and exaltation. I sing and think how the belly ranks up there with the great universals: love, death, and the changing of the seasons. Men also like them. My man tells me he likes mine, and he assures me his view is universal. To his knowledge there has never been a man on the plangent earth who got turned off by the female belly. Not a man who does not think of bellies by day and dream of them by night. Not a man who does not long to bury his face in the belly's roundness, to feel this spherical heaven with his hands, to raise his eyes to the vaulted dome of the belly's cathedral and gaze upon its hierarchy of angels and archangels.

Extravagant claims, but he makes his point. I see him on weekends and Wednesdays. Evening, and we loll in moonlight's mist. He is profligate, surrounding me like a nest, me, the egg of his affections. This is a man who gave up a lucrative medical practice to become a potter—except for two nights a week when he still works Emergency. I imagine him giving his full attention to a great belly-sized mound of clay, hefting it onto the wheel, turning it into a bulbous three-gallon jug with a narrow mouth. I imagine him imagining a woman who looks like me lifting it onto her head, walking down to the river.

"It's women who do the weaving and fire the crockery," I say. "Men should be sharpening spears. Fashioning tools."

"I was as good at mud pies as any girl," he says. "Better. Mine had fluted edges."

If he sang, he'd be a bass. Now he speaks with urgency.

"Frankincense and myrrh," he declares. He intones these words into my belly's fatty tissue. "All this piled wholesomeness: a heap of wheat!"

"You stole that from Solomon," I say. But I believe him. It's his nature to praise extravagantly and to be brutally truthful. "Don't you have a single pair of shoes that aren't frumpy?" he said once. "Are you *trying* to look like Mother Teresa?"

Why would he lie about bellies?

Uh Oh Belly

After a morning of scales and the frilling of tremolo, I meet Frieda for lunch. We swore loyalty to each other when we were in ponytails. Today we convene at the salad bar down the street from the Center for the Elimination of Famine. Frieda runs marathons and the center. If she sang, she'd be a contralto, though she doesn't sing except in the shower. There's a sense of amplitude about her that the thatch of black hair reiterates. As though even in svelteness, she's a full bowl about to spill over. When she's not scoring a plan to save babies from starvation, she's cooking. Osso bucco, pasta with arugula, asparagus with hollandaise to die for. Crème brûlée. But she's a finicky eater. I stack up the macaroni salad, take two corn muffins. Frieda is sparing. Leafy greens, today, are all she will eat.

"Look at this," she says, grabbing a handful of her belly. "I called this morning and got the dope on liposuction."

"Are you serious?" I say. "What you've got there is magnificent presence."

Frieda does not take this as a compliment. She thinks I'm doing the friend thing, and I'm not convincing. "Look," she said. "It *sticks out.*"

"So wear something blousy and full. Throw a shawl across one shoulder and let it drape down in front."

Frieda looks at me as though she's reconsidering my application.

"It doesn't look neat. It looks messy."

Her tummy is the result of giving birth to twins, both just under seven pounds. The month before their delivery, Frieda's husband, Kenneth, now her ex, stood up each morning, came round to her side of the bed, took hold of both her hands, and pulled. "Heave ho!" he said, brightly. A whole lot of stretching of Frieda's belly went on during that last trimester, and though afterward she faithfully carried out a regimen of sit-ups and leg lifts, her belly had signed on for the duration. It's like a bowling trophy.

"Kenneth liked your belly, didn't he?"

"That was before I had a belly. Anyway, I'm not Kenneth."

"You're the one who, when I'm with you, they don't see me."

"Still," Frieda says. "I don't like it."

Frieda has never met my man, though sometimes I talk about him. Now I tell her how he worships the belly, how it turns him on. I chatter on, talking up the belly as asset.

"Don't tamper with the material," I say. "Don't try to rewrite Rossini. The belly's stock is shooting up. Promise you won't sell."

Demolition Belly

My daughter Tara makes tuna sandwiches in her kitchen, humming a song I don't recognize. I flip through her copy of *Self*. Slick photograph of young woman, Levi's and tank top, inside the arm of man, white shirt unbuttoned to navel. He turns toward her, admiring her starved look. You have the impression he thinks this girl's got her act together, meaning she doesn't eat breakfast or lunch. I imagine her closing her mouth with adhesive tape so she won't be tempted.

I look at Tara, slender but definitely not without appetite. Somehow she managed not to become obsessed with gauntness. How? Because, creationism notwithstanding, girls are held responsible for the belly's protuberance. Tummy crunches are recommended, and diets. And the production of girdling undergarments is up. Failing these, there are those who favor sucking the belly in, in order to diminish its dramatic potential. But how long can anyone actually contract this busy and capacious bulge? Ten seconds max. Then it will be necessary to breathe. And though it's theoretically possible to inhale and exhale while keeping the tummy tucked in, do not try to carry on a conversation. You gasp single syllables: yes! no! help!

Should you fail to extinguish the belly's flame, denial is in order. In that case, do not under any circumstances open a magazine. Its pages are mined with girls so skinny you feel faint. You need handcuffs to keep yourself from dialing 911.

Where oh where is the sane shore where we may loll as we are? Frieda wants to feed the starving world, but in regard to her own belly, it's as though she's joined the opposition.

Tara arrives with a plate for each of us, nicely hefty sandwiches, chips, a pickle. "Look at this girl," I say, pointing to the page. "Is she anorexic, or what?"

"The tummy's been airbrushed out," Tara says. "They do the same thing to faces, landscapes. Airbrush is the name of the design game."

"But who did this airbrushing? The photo designer? Or the girl with her tablespoon of cottage cheese?"

Executive Committee for the International Year of the Belly

Frieda and I arrive at the pool just after Prenatal Water Aerobics. I've coaxed her here in the hope of seducing her into belly appreciation. You have to do the same thing for people who aren't sure they want to listen to opera. You explain how recitative works, give them little whiffs of bel canto, sit them down in the middle of a gorgeous aria. With Frieda today I'm trying for gospel. The overpowering heft of Sweet Honey in the Rock.

Upwards of twenty pregnancies converge in the dressing room. They comprise the continuum from modest to bulbous. Frieda and I sit amidst incubation.

"They ought to give us trophies," says the third-trimester ice skater, looking down at her convex navel.

A blonde with translucent skin regards her. "You're at least a nine," she says.

The door opens, and The Most Pregnant of All enters, holding up her belly, fingers laced so she won't drop it. Two others rush to her, usher her to a bench. Even seated she dares not let go of it. She's the Brandi Chastain of bellies.

"Olympic," I whisper.

Frieda scowls. "Fine, if you're pregnant," she mutters. "But I'm not."

I don't let Frieda bring me down. Notwithstanding my donations to Planned Parenthood and Zero Population Growth, I appreciate all this assertive extrusion. It's like sitting in a field of giant boulders engaged in deep breathing. Frieda is my friend, and I want her happiness. I imagine a transparent bubble around her through which harm cannot penetrate. Inside this bubble I decree she shall enjoy the small pleasures without anxiety: a chaise, an espresso, an umbrella of sunlight. Let a few flies buzz around the fruit plate—that's OK. And if leaves fall into the pool's clarity, no problem. They can be lifted out with a net. But let there be no anxiousness about bellies. Give the belly a shell necklace, a hula skirt. Give it a bikini bottom. Give it chocolate mousse.

"So we're not pregnant," I say. "But doesn't it make you feel validated? We did this: that's why we've got bellies. We gave at the office. We served our country."

Frieda frowns. She's the daughter of Puritans. It's like having a gene for self-criticism. All fleshy protuberances are suspect, and there's no such thing as leaving the church. Renounce the faith, but they'll find it in your DNA.

"Think of your babies," I say. "Your belly was their palace of Versailles."

"Next you'll suggest I open it to the public," Frieda says, "give guided tours."

Great Mother Belly

My man, I say. Though if I were interviewed by Charlie Rose, I'd say I don't believe in possessiveness. The more love in the world, the better, I'd say, or some such idealistic flag waving. Of course more love in the world translates to sleeping around. But jealousy is opportunity. I'd concede the primacy of jealousy, how it haunts the uncertain psyche, how it obsesses the obsessed. How it can pick up a couple and hurl them down: all those shimmering smithereens. Jealousy is universal, I'd say. But we can't live without it. It's our drug of choice. How else keep the edge of desire sharpened?

Let Charlie chew on that.

How would I actually feel if my man went running around with another woman? Tell the truth here! Yes, I'd feel a frisson of jealousy. Does she have more pert, more enticing nipples? Does he prefer the shape of her calf to mine? Does she flirt at length, stringing it out, or is she in a hurry to get down and dirty? But soon this itemizing would lose its allure. I'd shrug. *Whatever.* If I wanted a dog to lead around on a leash, I'd get one.

My man proposed monogamy, but I demurred. A contract cuts the grass, prunes the bushes. Installs a security system, the kind that turns on the lights when a stranger walks past. Suddenly romance has become a summit meeting, and you've turned into Milosevic and Madeleine Albright.

My man enjoys terrorizing himself with imaginary betrayal. Tonight he begs me to tell him again how once I failed to keep our date and spent the night with Harold instead. I didn't spend the night with Harold, though I thought about it hard. I'm good at fantasy though. So good that there are times when I almost forget it didn't really happen. I make up smoky details, wet and slippery scenery. Play up how my resolve weakened, how my panties got wet just talking to Harold across the table. I'm good at the Harold story. Even I get high on it. And my man gets turned on. He makes those sounds you make when you're dying from pleasure and at the same time covering your eyes and pushing it away. No! you shout. Yes!

Afterward, we lie on our backs, holding hands. Then he turns sideways and lays his ear against my belly, as though this fleshy mound with a blip in the middle might burst into song.

"What you've got here," he says, "is the Holy Grail!"

He kisses my navel, many kisses one after another. Clearly my belly is more than my belly. He's invested this ordinary puff of skin and fat and muscle over gut with deep meaning. To him it's the Blarney stone, Christ's wound, which Teresa of Avila wanted to kiss.

"There ought to be a temple to the belly," he says. "Incense, votaries. Great bells, tolling across plazas. The Vatican!"

I feel like a reincarnation of the Venus of Willendorf. Now there's a belly.

Marcella's Belly In Particular

Frieda and Marcella and I saw a lot of movies in high school, passing the popcorn back and forth. We shot baskets out of doors on sunny days. We talked about which boys were possible and how to avoid the rest. Now Marcella has a monument of a belly, and she celebrates it by taking it to the beach. Frieda and I stand on the boardwalk, scanning for that chocolate mound.

"There," Frieda says. "Between that mother with her kid and that guy, sleeping."

Marcella has laid her belly down, flanked by the two halves of her bikini, and oiled it. Now she offers it to the sun.

We pick our way between the bodies. The man asleep next to Marcella wakes up, looks at her navel, the highest point on the horizon. He is disoriented. Where is the water? The little kid—boy? girl?—comes with bucket and shovel and dribbles a tiny handful of sand into Marcella's navel. Marcella opens her eyes, sees the kid. She laughs. Sits up. The kid watches her heave herself onto all fours. She stands, walks toward the ocean.

Frieda and I arrive with our towels. The man smiles and moves over, making room. I notice him noticing the white side of Frieda's thigh, the curve where her hip reaches up to announce the belly. His curly salt and pepper ponytail bound with a rubber band. Frieda turns shyly away.

"Put some of this on me," Frieda says, handing me her sunscreen.

"Turn your back," I say. She does. Now she's facing the man. Discreetly he looks toward the water.

Me, I've never been good at denial. My talents lie in the opposite direction. I like to imagine things that aren't necessarily there but might be. Frieda's hair fans out around her like a Bedouin's tent in the desert. This man could make of her an exotic fantasy, and fast. He lies down on his back and closes his eyes. I imagine he imagines Frieda's belly is an oasis in the Sahara, a font of sacred water to which the faithful troop. They arrive, fall on their knees, reach up in awe to touch her belly. He imagines its white, veined nakedness: that nave, that sanctum.

Frieda too may be fantasizing. What a kick, she thinks, not to be thinking like Jonathan Edwards. To hell with original sin. If I'm going to be a sinner, at least don't tell me I was born that way. Let me have the credit.

I think I ought to leave these two alone. So I heave up, go down to the water, stand in a rill of surf. Chat up Marcella.

Marcella, showing off her ferocious, Roman Colosseum of a belly.

Brief History of the Belly in Painting

Rembrandt got it.

I take Frieda to see his *Danae*. The Danae reclines on her left side, propped on an elbow, right hand reaching out to greet the man who is about to step into the frame. Her attitude is voluptuous confidence. Light falls from above onto her shoulder, her thigh, onto her hip from which the belly hangs suspended. So protuberant is this belly that it shadows the inner thigh below it and the couch below the thigh. Shadowing that evokes mysteries, hiddenness, the belly's secrets. Secrets that Rembrandt welcomes. His take is triumphant. Hail to the splendorous halls of this palace of roundness! Hail to its great shouting mass!

Frieda's face is a struggle. She would like to believe there's a man close by who will love her belly with Rembrandt's erotic gusto. A man with the intelligence—and passion!—to throw himself down before the leaping flame at the center of the tabernacle.

"About the belly," I say, "they were never wrong, the old masters."

Frieda frowns. "Standards of beauty have changed."

"Standards of sexiness haven't," I say. "Some things are universal. Any man who doesn't get the glory of the belly isn't worthy of even your polite attention. Which reminds me. What about that guy you met at the beach?"

Freda waves this away with her hand.

"I made an appointment for August," Frieda says.

"With the guy?"

She shakes her head. "Liposuction."

"You're going to pay money to get rid of your belly?" I say. "When you're already a Rembrandt and it's free?"

Belly Paradox

Earth shifts toward dusk. I walk to the deli. Through the swinging door. What is it about swinging doors that makes you feel you're entering a place of no return? I pick up milk, some French roast. There's Frieda, down an aisle, deciding between a long, slender eggplant and one tending toward roundness. She chooses the long thin one. Nests it in her basket amidst cheeses, a loaf of bread. Why is it that more often than not beautiful women don't like the way they look? I like looking at Frieda. Why doesn't she?

From a side aisle a man approaches her, holding high a bottle that looks like Merlot.

"Found it!" he says.

It's the man I've been referring to as my man.

"Oh good," Frieda says.

Mine! Mine! I think. The butterfly heart flitters its wings.

Or is the heart an obese truck driver wanting yet another doughnut?

He lays the wine beside the eggplant. Then, from behind, he embraces Frieda. His left arm circles her waist, and with his right hand he reaches around and cups her belly.

This is a hand that could hold five pomegranates. It could hold a small bowl of goldfish. It could hold the sacrificial head of a goat. A great Hubbard squash harvested at sunset on the day of the autumnal equinox. I watch my man's hand, its appreciative greediness for her magnum opus. His face, in profile, looking down over her shoulder, smiling at his hand, the way his hand momentarily possesses such deliciousness. Frieda's face in mild ecstasy, as though his simple, charged gesture has vastly expanded her capacity for pleasure.

I step discreetly out of sight. Go to the register, pay. Head for that swinging door. How right I was about that door. I walked in complacent as your average heifer. Now get it, I tell myself. The woman walking out is the new you. Quivering wavelets of uncertainty, bordered by a ten-foot concrete wall set with the jagged glass of broken Cerveza bottles. What was all that politically correct blabber about more love in the world? Some fatuous diatribe about the honing of desire's edge?

I had, back there, a bowl of buttered popcorn, and it was all mine!

The sky leans into black. Two stars. This is where Charlie Rose would probe.

You feel jealous? he'd say, his blue eyes flashing with relish.

It was good to be reminded that I think of him as my man, I say. People aren't furniture. You try to love the hard parts.

Charlie hunches down and leans toward me, zeroing in.

So you are just a little bit jealous?

Actually I'm really, really jealous, I say. Olympic medal jealous, if you want to know.

So what are you going to do? Charlie says.

I keep walking. You have to admire my man, I say. If I'd tried to arrange it, if I'd coached him myself, then planted him in her life, I couldn't have got it as right as he's got it on his own.

I try humming a new air I've lately composed in honor of the belly. There's a suggestion of a quaver. Charlie hears it. He gets that look in his eyes: gotcha! Keep going, I tell myself. Just keep on walking into the present.

Frieda will flourish in the hands of my man, I say. He'll worship at her shrine, pile lilies on the altar. Her belly will become his golden calf. And under the force of his adoration her anxiety about her belly will evaporate. Frieda will assume her rightful throne, her crown. At least, that's what I hope. Though even such admiration as my man delivers may not be enough to sway Frieda from the centuries of belly hatred that have come down to us here.

It's you I'm asking about, Charlie says. You thought this guy was yours, and now he's running around with your best friend.

Frieda doesn't know he's my man, and he doesn't know she's my friend. I've never introduced them. But he's exactly what I've been hoping would happen to Frieda.

Except that he's betrayed you.

What's important? I say. Having a dog on a leash or putting more love into the world?

That's your canned rhetoric showing, Charlie says.

Maybe it is, I say. But my man's like Rembrandt. He gets it. I love that about him.

I'm waiting, Charlie says.

I take two deep breaths.

I remind myself there is a thing people do, women and men, when they fall in love. They get swept up into the swirl of erotic desire, and it's like a conversion. They forget you who were their best, their most loyal friend. They don't have time for so much as a single phone call. Which is good, because if they were actually to phone you, you would recognize at once that this was a duty call, and you would feel way worse than you already do.

You've been abandoned—yes! No euphemisms here!

You go into damage control mode. You remind yourself that obsession renders desire even more delicious than it already was. And you tell yourself the cruddy ambience imposed upon you really has nothing to do with you personally. It's all about the two of them, and they can't help it. They're temporarily berserk, inside a hurricane where the rules of weather don't apply. They will toss their entire wardrobes into the trash and go on a shopping spree they'll be paying interest on for months, but they think it's worth it. You remind yourself that down the road a piece there will come a moment when both of them understand that the other is fatally flawed. But until that time you're about as interesting to your former pal as a canceled check.

Get used to it, I tell myself. You're here outside the deli for the duration. And this too shall pass. Go sing some arias about the female belly, and keep practicing those scales.

I take a third deep breath. Listen, Charlie, I say. It's like these socks Frieda and Marcella bought me once for a birthday joke. One sock says, My boyfriend ran off with my girlfriend. The other sock says, I'm going to miss her.

HERACLITUS, HELP ME

I

Heraclitus, you who are wise. *Everything flows,* you say. *Nothing abides.* I sit, and Mary Cassatt's paintings float before me, and there you are again, my daughter, in the paintings, in your sweet baby flesh, and I am with you. You were Cassatt's *Sleepy Nicole,* the ethereal drowsy baby, arms around my neck, head on my shoulder, my arms curves of peach light. I surrounded you: I was drunk on your milky, powdery sweetness.

When a woman's inside that love with her child, their love feels eternal. The two lives are one being, an endless touching. I bathed in your light, you in mine. See, in *The Child's Bath* the mother burnishing her daughter's tiny foot with water. See the sheen of the mother's striped dress, the softened folds of a towel. See the satin riffles of the water.

It throws apart, says Heraclitus, *then brings together again.* The throwing apart was a tear across serene afternoon. It happened suddenly, your going. A violent going, your gesture a shock, a sudden whiteness in the air. But there has to be violence, Heraclitus says, when I go to him with my swollen eyes and my questions. All right, yes, but what I did not know was that your going would be my doing. That the violence would be mine.

And now: what do I do now that you're gone? I don't have to go to the store—whom would I buy food for? We need only a little food now, he and I. I have only a few dishes to wash. Still I run the water in the sink, add soap. Should I leave him and start over? Find a house where light pours in like your light once poured onto me endlessly? I imagine the room where I would sit in chartreuse light, feeling the green warmth on my skin. I look for any little bit of happiness that I can blow on, breathe into. And I tell myself I must give myself to change, its movement, even when that movement is violent. And then there is Mary Cassatt. When you look at one of the paintings, you see the coming together. You don't see the shock of the throwing apart.

See our green shimmering, you and I, rocking inside the great body. I had what I wanted, and I imagined I would always have it. You were here, born into the world. I would never again be a woman without a child. This was fixed, indestructible, a fact. Of course you'd grow up and go out from me, go away. But that would be organic, a natural part of the process. And in that going I would not lose you: you would always be mine, and I yours.

For I had become a woman with a child.

I had crossed over.

When you could sit up, I helped you drink from a cup. We were Cassatt's *Mother Feeding Child*. Girl on the mother's lap, the glass at the level of the mother's chiffon breast. Think of the blue veins beneath the skin of that breast, the mother's and the child's cheeks ruddy from their walk in the sun. The mother's hand, above the little hands, steadying the glass. Pie on our plate. Pitcher the color of sky.

After we'd eaten, you looked up. My hands laced around your belly, your arm on top of my arm, your head thrown back against my billowing shoulder. And I admit I bowed down before your beauty. It's bad to worship idols, but I worshipped you. Nothing but worship could slake me. I said yes, yes, yes, yes. I threw open the doors.

Light poured in, its warmth, its bronze. Of course light is impermanent—I know, Heraclitus, *nothing abides*—but light is also cyclic. This looking at you in the light would happen again and again. It would never not continue. That is what idolatry is: the idolater believes she and her object will not die.

But there has to be a death. Heraclitus said it another way: *There is exchange of all things for fire*. Fire lives in the death of air. Air has to die, air has to feed itself to the fire. I should have seen it coming. For this death began long before your going. It began almost at the beginning, when your body slipped out, became separate from mine. Birth was a little death, but I refused to see the death in it. Or perhaps I couldn't see it because your light blinded me.

One day he came and stood, looking down at us. Across our shimmering, lit green: his shadow. You had learned to walk, to talk. Your legs had grown long. When you sat on my lap, they hung down. People said we looked alike, you and I, but I couldn't see this. I saw only you, a child so beautiful I could not stop looking. I watched you eat; I watched you read. I watched you brush your hair. In the evening I watched you get tired. Before I went to bed I came and stood in the doorway and watched you asleep on your belly, head turned to one side, long hair swirled around your temples. How you went on, breath by breath. I stood there and stood there.

Then he came, and I imagined we would take us to him as one, you and I. For we were, you and I, one single vibration in the air.

But the phases of fire, Heraclitus, are as you say. They are craving and satiety. He came and stood, looking down, desiring me. He wanted to touch my body, to know it everywhere. And of course this was only natural. For my body, like yours, was beautiful. And I wanted him. I wanted to touch his body, to know it everywhere. I wanted him for both of us. I wanted him so that we might have that perfect thing, the family. I wanted to bind him to us with the binding of the body, to sew him into our sinew and bone.

Now we eat, he and I. Then one day, we're out of food. I go to the store. How much less we need now! No need to buy milk, your favorite cheese. I choose some bread you liked. A sweet red pepper for its color. And two avocados, because you and I like them, because in my imagination where the tiniest detail may be significant, I imagine that if I buy these avocados you may appear.

I lay the avocados side by side in the cart. I feel tired: it's an effort to stand. I used to have you with me, sitting in the cart, your knees against my belly, your legs swinging. I would lean over you, watching you eat a cookie. Now the magazines beside the checkout are too bright to look at. Still I lift one, leaf through, glance at the shiny clothes, the women's perfect faces. But there is no real charm in these magazines. These magazines have never seen you. These magazines don't know how to love.

Outside, the wind is blowing. Warm wind, a wind with spring in it. When you drank my breasts, I drank down the look of you, the fact of you drinking me. I had everything I wanted; I was full of my happiness, replete with it. Now I stand in the wind, holding a loaf of bread, two avocados.

I thought if I loved him enough and I loved you enough, we would become three in one.

But though I tried to pull you into the circle I made with him, your shadow fell between us. And when I tried to pull him into the circle I made with you, his shadow fell between us. I could only go away from him and come back to you, come away from you and go back to him. You kept asking, wanting, needing, hoping. He kept asking, wanting, needing, hoping.

The phases of the fire, says Heraclitus, *are craving and satiety*, oh yes. We are thrown back and forth between these two. I became like fire, flaring up for one of you and burning down, flaring up and burning down for the other. I who had been whole became a riven thing, two ragged halves of me, first one, then the other without resolution.

I ran to you and made a oneness with you, and then I ran to him and made a oneness with him. And still, darling, in my drive to love you completely, I also kept him out. Though he loved me, he felt abandoned. Though he entered me, he could not enter our oneness, yours and mine, and so he could not possess me completely. He rattled the gate; he pushed; he pulled. He did not give up. His gaze kept coming. He kept trying. And you and I closed our shimmering, pulling it closer around us, so that he stood alone, outside.

This is why he does not appear in Mary Cassatt's paintings. Because, darling, you and I were one.

And yet when I ran to him, you felt abandoned. And I saw your face change. In *Child in a Straw Hat*, the hat belongs to the little girl's mother. The girl's little face is dwarfed by the huge crown, so that her face, in the hat, looks drowned. The brim is utterly straight: uncompromising. She is given no quarter. Her honey gold hair is unkempt, heightening her look of desolation. Her small full mouth crimps with worry, and she clasps her hands together. She sees the temple in ruins, the shadow on the grass.

A pink pinafore over a white blouse accents her helplessness. How impossible it is, in pink, to think of saving oneself, and yet she must, for there is no one to help her.

Quickly I pulled you to me, kissed your hair. I whispered our secret words. I caressed your small shoulders.

And still in spite of my longing to comfort you, shadow fell across our green shoots.

Had I not looked at the paintings carefully? Had I not seen their essence? But that essence has to be shattered. It has to be ripped. Torn. Paintings are true, but only for a moment. Then they are false.

Heraclitus, I see this now. But I could not see it then.

Cool things become warm; the warm grows cool. You were hurt by my going to him, and I was hurt by your hurt. You came to me and wept. I also wept. You begged me to take us away from him. And I wanted to go away, because I could scarcely bear our throwing apart, yours and mine.

But I could not go away from him. For now I had bound him to me. And it is not easy to undo a binding. A binding may wear away, but that is not the same as undoing a binding.

And so, darling, it began to be visible, our throwing apart, yours and mine: though I did not want to see it, it began.

And I was the one who had begun it.

Each time I left him, I tried to return to you and not to see the throwing apart beginning. That you were there made me happy, even in the midst of unhappiness. I came and went, went and came, and I kept believing that soon our shimmering sphere would surround him with its heat. Our lit sphere would warm him and warm us, and you and he would loosen the hard single-ness of your gazes and take the other in.

You were both hot with jealousy, angry with your wanting of my body.

Then you grew cool. You were cold now. You would not take off your sweater. The starlight at night seemed obscured by cloud. Now when I came to you, I could not get close to you. You sheathed yourself in the small warmth of your sadness. I could not find a way through it to where you were.

You pulled sadness around you like that sweater, and I stood outside.

I saw your face, and I understood I had failed. I had failed to get you to love the man, and I had failed to pull away from him. It was as though I had torn our sphere, yours and mine, with my hands.

It was as though I had ripped our single skin with my teeth.

Thus, in the turning of a moment—a silver bowl held up and turned, slightly, in the light—I learned anguish.

II

You grew tall in that body of your own, and your flesh blossomed. Your body began to resemble my body. I knew that the time of your departure was coming. And I had hoped your going would happen gradually, the way it happens for other mothers, so gradually I'd hardly notice.

Heraclitus warned me that it would not happen that way, but I did not want to understand.

The thunderbolt, he said, *pilots all things*. The man's paper-weight was igneous. Dark, clotted glass, mass from which no light could escape. One evening, in the midst of arguing with him, you understood. If you could not win me from him, you would at least save yourself. I heard your two voices rising toward fury, and I came and stood in the doorway. Two voices, like pointing fingers. Then your anger rose up like a swell of water becoming huge just before it crashes onto sand. From this green wave, I watched your white arm thrust up. I watched you hurl the black paperweight.

There it went in an arc, your thunderous bolt, your gleaming gesture.

Though it did not hit him, you had struck. On the power of that gesture you were gone.

Hear me, Heraclitus: I wake in the dark, sobbing. I sob and sob, drenched in every cell.

What can I do? the man asks.

Hold me, I say, and he tries. But no one can hold a wave. I am a surge of water, rising and falling. Each sob throws my body down, then heaves it up again. I am consumed in this being taken and taken. Afterward I fall onto my back, gasping.

The silence after grief is placid water. I drift there. I float. Then I see that I have failed in this sobbing. Nothing is built forward, nothing is forged.

I began this sobbing with nothing.

And now I still have nothing.

He begs me to lie down with him. I let him lead me to the bed. I hurl my body toward him. I try to forge something that will hold me, but my heart is blank. I turn on my side, away from him. He puts his arm around me, to comfort me. I feel his arm, but I cannot feel comfort. My body is everywhere disconsolate. I hope he won't talk to me, not right now.

I get up, go into the kitchen and pretend to cook. I make my body busy, so he won't talk to me. I can't pay attention to him, not now. I can't keep my mind on what he says. Once we shared concerns, he and I, but now I have only one concern. I am fascinated by it. I can't tear myself from it. Like oxygen, I have to have it.

It is my anguish.

III

Then I am given a gift: you telephone. You would like to meet me. How long has it been since you left? A week? Two weeks? An eon. Two eons. We agree to meet the next day. So, I think. Something will happen, but what? Is there a way you and I can be, again, one body?

Is there a way again, that we can enter again the tenderness of the great body around us?

How faded the man seems now, sitting alone. I feel a wave of kindness toward him. But I don't go to him. He cannot satisfy my longing for you. He cannot replace you as the object of my attention. I believe he would do almost anything for me. But he can't provide the one thing I most need: your light, streaming across space.

How sad the man must be, and then angry, to be just now superfluous. To have to stand at the edges and wait to be noticed. But this is how it is in the paintings. Mother and child feed each other. They make the light together. All that is necessary in the paintings is the mother and child. He is not there because he has nothing we need.

You phone again. You delay. I must wait three more days. I wait three more days. I do things, things I can't remember doing. When that day arrives, I go through the time called morning and the time called noon. I go through the time called early afternoon.

Finally I bathe; I dress. I go to meet you. Do I notice the new leaves shining beside the path? I walk, imagining the tea shop, how we will sit in a sunlit room.

My body has become a trajectory, motion whose destination is you. The tea shop comes into view, and you. I see your face filling with expectation, and I feel a sweep of hopefulness across my skin. We embrace, briefly. We find a table, sit. We look at each other. It's as though we are feasting again, eating each other's bodies. A young woman takes our order, but I hardly see her. I am looking at your face, as you look at mine. We are fastened on this meal.

The young woman brings our tea. My mind is busy calculating hours and distances. I measure how two weeks without seeing you might feel, and I reassure myself: these distances are not so great, these durations are bearable. We drink, we eat, just as we used to, yet not as we used to.

You tell me that it was time for you to go, that you understood you needed to go. But how hard it was, you say, how hard to go. You did not know how to leave me. The only way you could imagine to leave me was to grasp the black paperweight and pull back your white arm.

I watch you sitting before me now, my darling, and in quick, instinctual knowing, I understand. I know now what you will say.

Your argument with him, you say, was merely your excuse.

It was me you had to leave, I say.

Yes, you say. It was you I had to leave.

I gaze at your body across from me, you body that is continuously changing, even as I gaze. Now I am able to see how it might have been, your gradual, natural pulling away. How little by little you had run out of the green sphere more often, stayed away longer. Though of course this gradual, natural going isn't in the paintings.

What can be painted would require three paintings. One painting of the two of us together, one painting of me, alone, and one painting of you, also alone.

The paintings show only before, and after. For the moment of throwing apart is that invisible shift that cannot be painted.

The paintings are paintings of discrete moments. I had that, for a little while, that handful of scattered moments. You can be there for a moment: then nothing abides.

IV

There is an intelligence, Heraclitus says, *by which all things are steered through all things. Thus fire lives in the death of air; water lives in the death of fire.* How is it that we forget the great touching, the way it arcs through everything, the way it takes everything without judgment, without hesitation?

Now here you are, daughter, upright in your body, shining, going on. I see you now without anguish in Cassatt's *Young Woman Sewing in the Garden.* There you sit, full-bodied, in your white dress, threading a needle amidst the red poppies. In that painting you are not with me inside our shimmering. Our shimmering is gone now, and your hair is pulled back the way grown women pull it back and fasten it. You are off by yourself, making your own light, a rosy gold. You have survived my ignorance. You have survived my violence. The red poppies flare around your knees.

You and I, daughter, were once a single being, and I will remember that. But now I will leave you, as you left me, like fire having consumed the air of your being, and you, glad to give yourself to me, to let me consume. And you, you were the water that drank my fire, and now you have drunk me. Now, darling, forgive me. Forgive me, so that I may also forgive myself.

Heraclitus, I see this now as I could not understand it before. What is beautiful in the paintings is not, as I had thought, exclusive. For there is no exclusion. There is only the ceaseless moving of the two energies within the great body. The two energies of the throwing apart and the coming together again.

And in our shining, mother and child, we embodied that great body. So that by loving each other already we loved the man even before we knew him. Already we included him.

Heraclitus, wise counselor, hear me now. I want to be taken back into that great body. Here now I let go of the anguish of throwing apart—let it go like casting a painting into the river. Let that painting slide easily away on the water and in a moment drift from sight.

AIR, A ROMANCE

Who thought this up?!
The lover visible
and the Beloved invisible!
    —Rumi

Air, that elusive whiff of a female, balancing on the hint of a toe, turns, flips her gossamer whirl of skirt, and wafts off, leaving him

standing there. Just when he thought he'd got his word ducks in quite a nifty row. Just when he was (breezily, he hoped) nudging his eloquence in her direction, hoping to surround her with breathy badinage so interesting she wouldn't be able to resist. He, igneous, plutonic granite, the very essence of a stolid presence, for whom the bottom line is Rock-of-Gibraltar-in-the-Grip-of-Gravity materiality. To whom talk represents everything tantalizing and beyond him, for whom every utterance is effort, like lifting and placing one stone on top of another until one has built, substantially, a monument.

  He'd waited for her to speak, but she'd seemed shy. So he'd forged ahead, with the idea that this pursing of his lips to produce profundities would power him closer, and there they would be, his words—and hers, whispering wisps—suspended, while the two of them together finessed a rather different structure. He thought his efforts would lead, eventually, to the air brush of a kiss, or at the very least a near miss. But there she goes, only the back of her heels showing, so that he has to will himself after her, and then her trail through the woods turns a corner, and she's

gone. He's reduced to silence.

Silence is final, except when it's pregnant, but this one isn't.

Isn't that a hint of her perfume, wafting past in the space where she'd been? This hint of fragrance is all that's left of her. Inside he feels, well, uniformly massive: the material form of emptiness. What's the point of talking to oneself? It takes two, he thinks, and he would like the two to be himself and Air. When Air is there, then and only then is true intercourse possible.

Meanwhile, Air has had it. All that pomposity! If only he'd dance instead of talk! But he is not light on his feet. Fluency and fluidity, she thinks, flitting off, are to the point: counterpoint to his weighty pronouncements. She goes out over the lake's soft dampness. Cool, she lingers there, gazing down. Handsome dragonflies dive and swerve above the fiery lilies. The lilies float, and in floating seem to breathe, their petals rising a little, then settling,

then rising. But here come the other airs, in groups of twos and threes, followed by those formidable elders, the winds. In this breathy sphere above the lake they assemble, airs of all nations, winds of the four directions, hovering above the lilies' perfumed aspirations. See how they inspire each other! They have gathered to conspire together to carry out a worldwide whispering campaign, the thrust of which is a spray of separate but interpenetrating propositions: all of which come down to eschewing leaden verbiage and promoting universal lightness in all things.

And now—no need to call things to order, since a lazy disorder is the order of their day. Let the proceedings begin.

Platforms: To infuse politicians with the spirit of truth. To convince smokers to take up phrana breathing. To call into question the arbitrariness of all boundaries. To arrange symposia at which enemies vent gently, then negotiate lightly. To use airy speech and inspired story to diffuse hostilities. To inspire poets, provide philosophers lucidity, collaborate with earthworms in aeration and birds in nest construction. To promote the possibility of flight even in unlikely species. To liberally spread invisible tranquility. And generally to infuse seriousness with levity.

All platforms pass in a jiffy. There is hilarity, much applause, and breezy embracing. One by one airs and winds disperse. The lilies sigh and begin to settle in for evening. Air floats toward shore, imagining a pungent and refreshing sail through the firs. And there he is

leaning against a trunk: sunk down, immovable. Granite, slumped (if granite could). She diagonals down. To get his attention, she rills her frilly skirt cancan in front of him.

—There are uses for your practiced phrases, she says. —We need you on the Convincing Committee at the next Plenary on Air Pollution. But you must be light-tongued! And you must be brief, though also charmingly persistent. Make your speech weightless, though not frivolous. Come straight to the point, but deftly and succinctly, as in a pirouette. Be convincing, avoid mincing, and whatever you say, be not tedious,

and do not run up a flag!

Granite looks at her, astonished. How sweetly she's admonished him. He feels suddenly—can it be?—necessary after all.

And tall, suddenly, instead of bulky, and, happily, less ponderous but more magnificent. Her breathiness, fluttering before him, has had the effect of gradually inflating him. Imagine! It's as though at last he has room to breathe, and is that *her* breath or his he's breathing? Without a thought for the consequences, he reaches out to pull her to him—

but what's that whirring, like the wings of a summer swan startled, taking flight?

Quickly, lightly, she's gone again, west this time, across the water toward that rosy span of clouds, leaving him not bereft exactly, but, for Granite, actually, well,

inspired. The idea that he might play a part, however small, in improving Air's affairs thrills him. He feels expansive! Yes! Even almost for him—*fluid*. He watches what he thinks may be her in the distance. What to do? Accept her maddening hazy, blurry, fuzzy, misty, filmy imperceptibility?

Or is the question not what to do but who to be? (*Is* that her in the distance, hovering over Earth Our Mother?) But be what? Can he ever, possibly, actually become

her rock solid, clearly visible, absolutely hard, immovable lover?

III

MITOSIS

*The mound had been inside her from the begin-
ning. Perhaps she'd seen it jutting up above flat land when she held her
mother's hand to walk to the river? Or had she seen it when her father
picked her up and carried her? Or was the feeling of being carried from
before her birth, when the part of her father that would become part of
her was still inside him? At that time the prophet had begun the mound,
but it was not yet as tall as ten men.*

*I remember women and men throwing mud onto the mound, she'd
told her father, when the mound was no taller than a small baobab.*

*That was before the British bombed it with their airplane, he'd
said. Even I was not born then. Her father folded his long legs and took
her on his lap. He moved slowly out of a thoughtful gentleness toward the
world. Someday we'll go there, he said. You'll see it.*

I have seen it, she said. Now it's inside me.

I

It was because of the road stretching ahead in shimmering
heat that this baby was eating what was left of her body. He
sucked Ayak's empty breast and cried—cries like small rips. The

women walked north. There, it was said, pink *Turuks* gave food. Three years the *raau* fields had languished in drought. The first bad year men traveled north to Khartoum to work, and women ate next year's seed grain and slaughtered a cow. The second year the cows were too thin to stand up by themselves. The women gathered wild grain and fed their children every other day. Now it was the third year. They'd picked leaves. They'd torn away branches and pounded these in a mortar and cooked them. They'd cut up their leather skirts and boiled the bits in water.

Ahead a single baobab rose from flat scrub. They stopped in its shade. People hollowed out the trunks of baobabs to make a tank to store water. Ayak had gone with her father to the baobab, climbed the tree and filled the bucket, then lowered it. This baobab, though, had no water, so the women drank from a pool in the dried river bed. How can we sleep now, she thought, like an animal without skin? How can we live broken in pieces?

They rested and then stood and began to walk. Ahead they could see a cluster of acacias where there might be more water. But when they stood beneath the yellow blossoms there was no water. Ayak's baby began to cry again. The road had made this child, she thought, and now the road should take it. But when they started walking, she did not lay the baby down. One small boy refused to go on. His mother had one child strapped to her back, and in a sling a baby. Get up! she told him. We are going. When he did not raise his eyes, his mother walked on. But there came a point when she turned and walked back to him, laid the baby on the ground, picked up the boy, and started walking.

As a child Ayak had imagined the road had always been there. She knew that sometimes a trader from the north brought salt and tobacco, and in the town she'd see two pink *Turuks* who brought their god and built this thing, a church. But that northerners had been coming on the road for years to take slaves, that Brits and

Egyptians had partitioned Sudan into north and south and then gone, leaving northerners to rule—these were facts she had not been told. Or if she'd heard her father say these things to another man, she'd paid no attention.

The road seemed to have always been there like the baobabs where the Dinka stored water. What was important was the rhythm of people's lives braiding with the lives of cows. This rhythm was made not just of time and the sky but also of winds and things of earth which you could touch. Also there were things you could not touch, things which happened inside this rhythm. Even when a feud broke out and the men fought, the rhythm held the men together.

Ayak carried water and gathered firewood. She helped her mother, Kwei, churn butter and clean the cattle's byre. The blue wind kept weaving the globe of the world, and her body felt as sleek as those white storks flashing their black and red bills in the river's shallows. Heat sprouted her father's *raau* seeds, and every morning when the sun was an ox turning the wheel of heat, Ayak and Patal walked with the other children to take the cattle to the place of lush grass. They walked brushing against the cows, drifting in the shifting sway of the heifers' bodies. When sun rang the bell of noon, Ayak held her father's heifer Chol by the nostrils and spoke softly, and Patal squirted milk into the gourd.

He was slender like those storks, and he moved with a stately deliberation. "Cows," he said, "are sent down from the sky. We are drinking the sky's body."

They passed the gourd back and forth. Then they rested beneath an acacia. A breeze brushed down pale yellow petals.

"Once an old woman walked to the river," Patal said. His voice beginning a story was tinder catching and burning. "She knelt to draw water, and when she leaned far over, the god in the river saw her. He was lonely, and he wanted a woman to play with. I will give her a child even though she is old, he thought, and then she will stay with me. So the god rose up and pulled her in and floated the seed for a child into her belly.

"When people saw the child growing inside an old woman, they knew this child would be a prophet. When the child was born, he had a full set of teeth, and immediately he began to talk. The boy knew when a person was lying, and he knew when a bad wind was coming. When soldiers were coming, he told people to run away quickly. His mother took him every day to the river to talk to his father, but she was very old, and one night she died. The son took her body to the river and gave her back to the water. But without his mother he was unhappy. So the next day he came and said, Take me too, for I miss my mother. Then he plunged in, and the god turned him back into water. Now he and his mother live with the god in the river."

When Patal told stories, she became a glistening. The women who gathered at his mother's hut also wanted stories. Sometimes he made people laugh. Sometimes a story turned the elders around him solemn. Boy with the tongue, they called him.

Chol bellowed. The blue wind in its moaning weaving of all things had made this heifer big with calf. She bellowed again, her tail arched, and the slick calf slipped out. They watched Chol's tongue lick the calf clean. Ayak's father's name was Akol. Now she thought of another name: Marial. Two names, a sound and its echo.

"Marial," she said. "Marial will be his name."

They helped Chol nose Marial up. He found the udder and drank. Heat had piled and piled like great stones. When the sun began to take these stones down, Ayak lifted Marial onto her shoulders and carried him.

"I want to get a baby prophet from the river god," she said. "How can I do that?"

"The story says the god floated the seed into her. If I can find a way, I'll help you."

———

Ayak looked into Marial's eyes one morning and realized that Marial was as tall as she was. That was the day the blue wind brought the missionary's wife to teach them paper. Clarissa wore a hat over her red hair to shade her pink *Turuk* face. Clarissa: her name hissed like a snake. But she was benign as the grey sand grouse nesting on the ground.

"Among you tall, thin Dinka," Clarissa said, "this grouse looks quite fat—like me."

Clarissa's breeze riffled the heat. She taught them to write numbers and words on paper. And in her science book they saw this small, invisible thing called a cell.

"The cell's nucleus is like a seed," Clarissa said. "It splits into two parts and by this dividing makes more of itself. And this dividing and multiplying are happening everywhere—in grass, in cows, in people's bodies. It's how things grow." She paused. "We call this 'mitosis.'"

Mitosis—the dividing and the two parts growing. It was how Marial had grown inside Chol. How Ayak had grown inside her mother, Kwei. Mitosis: how the gods made more of things. After class she and Patal walked Clarissa to the road. Clarissa told them the story of the Virgin Mary. She said that a woman couldn't make a child alone. A man had to give her a baby. Though it was God himself who gave Mary the Christ child.

"In Patal's story," Ayak said, "the river gives the mother a baby prophet. Tell her."

Patal's words spread like a stork's wings and floated the story into Clarissa's ears.

"What a wonderful storyteller you are," she said. "You will be able to write down these stories so that the British can read them." She slung her arms around their shoulders. "Did you know that this road was made by the British? We made it back in the time of the Madhi. That was when we kept the Madhi's *jallabahs* from coming south and stealing you to be their slaves."

———

On the branches of the baobab beside the river, brown parrots fluffed their pale chartreuse breasts and muttered, and Ayak and Patal did not know that the blue wind's weave was tearing the way a person sometimes tore a leaf bit by bit into pieces. They'd brought Marial with them to the baobab because they liked to lean against his belly to study. Patal's mother, Nyanthon, had said that the baobab had given him his tongue for stories. Nyanthon's hair was cropped short. She was round like a clay water jar and her eyes bright as the eyes of the tiger. When Patal was in my belly, she'd said, I came to the river and felt him wanting to come out. So I knelt and held onto the baobab, and he was born.

Marial's belly was warm as the earth at midday. She put her ear there and heard the sound of the many footsteps of the god Deng making Marial's cells divide and multiply.

"Spell 'mitosis,'" Patal said. "It's on the test."

Back and forth they repeated the names of each word's letters. Patal made a story about the letter O in mitosis. "It is a fat man standing between *mit* and *sis*, and he puts his arms around both—like Clarissa's arms over our shoulders."

Clarissa had told them that Christ came inside a British girl, and she fell on the ground. When she stood, she discovered that Christ had taught her to read. People walked from far away to hear her read from a book like a prophet. Ayak thought of the Dinka game in which a girl went on her knees in the center of the children's circle. The children beat their laps and sang, and the girl beat the ground with her hands and hopped and turned inside the circle. The singing and beating grew until the girl was swept up, possessed, her body jerking. Then a mother came and broke up the circle, and the children ran away laughing.

"Would you believe the words of a prophet like that girl?" Ayak said.

"Yes, because prophecy comes from Deng. Men can't decide it. Nyaruac was a girl prophet from the time of our grandparents.

My mother says Nyaruac cured cattle and took away pain from the belly of my grandmother. Then people brought Nyaruac butter and beer."

A parrot squawked and burst from the baobab. Ayak's father, Akol, was coming from his fields. He paused beneath the acacias and looked up at the laughing doves. The gods had sprinkled pale blue powder on their gray wings, and he liked to talk to them. He picked sprigs of acacia blossoms and gave one to each child.

Ayak brushed her sprig against her cheek. "Was I born beneath this baobab like Patal?"

Akol looked at the river sliding itself along. He thought of that other river where he had done a bad thing—a thing that was also good. He smiled. "My daughter is growing very tall."

He was the tallest man in the village. Her mother, Kwei, said Akol was the only man with legs long enough to outrun a lion. The lion will grow tired, she'd said, and say, That man is too thin. Give me a man with more meat.

"Ayak will be the tallest woman in the village," Patal said, "because you're her father."

He gave Ayak his acacia sprig so that she might brush pollen powder on both cheeks at once.

"I'm as tall as Marial," Ayak said. "Almost as tall as Clarissa." She thought of Clarissa's hat, its two ribbons hanging down in back. "Clarissa told us the British made this road."

"This road brings Clarissa to teach you paper. And this road also makes it easy for *jallabahs* to steal our cattle." Akol would not say to children that *jallabahs* also stole young girls and sometimes boys. Nor would he say that even Dinka and Nuer soldiers borrowed young girls for their pleasure. "Some things are both good and bad. *Jallabahs* steal our cattle, but we also steal. Nuer steal Dinka cattle, and sometimes we steal theirs. Then we fight each other when we should fight the *jallabahs* instead."

He'd been saying this as far back as Ayak could remember. The other men agreed. Then a Dinka man would say that some Nuer had come onto his grass and stolen cows, and the village men would go with him to fight the Nuer. Even her father went with them.

II

It was the red wind that tore a great hole in things and took Patal away. Ayak knew there'd been a war long ago between north and south, but she did not know that the edges had begun to fray again, like those papyrus mats her mother spread inside the *tukul*. Nor did she know that the north needed the south's rivers and wanted the grass, which hid pools of black oil. The blue wind, Kwei said, wove cattle, sky, and grass. But red winds tore the blue wind's weaving, each gust a spear hurtling through air.

"The red wind steals the south's good *gos*," Kwei said, "and blows it north. There it eats the north's dust, blows back south, and spits it out."

Nyanthon thrust out a cooking pot. "Look! Dust is what we are given to eat."

"When a hungry man in the north steals food," Kwei said, "*jallabahs* cut off his hand. And in Khartoum they say Deng is not a real god."

"The British say that too," Nyanthon said. "Then they give *jallabahs* guns. The north's leader came in a motor car wearing a safari suit and black glass over his eyes. He promised schools and a hospital. He took off the black glass and ate with us. Then he got in the motor car and went away. We never heard from him again."

"*Jallabahs* have been stealing us since the beginning of the world," Kwei said. "They think we are slaves because we let them take our people. Then those British said they would stop the stealing. But they made us build the road, and took our cows for their tax."

"We don't need a road," Nyanthon said. "We can go anywhere without one."

"You say that because we don't have motor cars," Kwei said. "When we get them, the road will be ours."

Patal was of age to take the forehead cuts that would make him a man.

"Are you sure you want this?" Clarissa said. "Someday you will come to my country, and there no men have this *gaar*."

"Do you prefer me with *gaar*," he asked Ayak, "or without?"

She hesitated. "I am half yes and half no."

He laughed. "This is how the world is now. Half north and half south, and you half no and half yes."

Clarissa laughed too. "You are both very smart with paper," she said. "And we are near the end of our books. It's time for both of you to go to the secondary school at Rumbek."

Their fathers and Nyanthon agreed, but Kwei would not part with her one daughter. Without you, Akol told Ayak, Kwei is the blossoms of acacia when they fall on the ground. Patal would return larger and multiplied, Ayak thought, and she too would multiply. But first they would have to divide.

The day he was to leave, she walked with him to the road.

"We are like a sheet of paper," she said, "that has been ripped in two."

"Don't worry. I will bring back my half of the paper."

The red wind's gusts shot across the river, tearing the riffles. Ayak saw the old heron woman standing in the water where four or five herons were feeding. She stood very still like a heron and made heron sounds. Slowly the herons came closer.

A gust hit the baobab, and the boughs moaned. Always now the mound was inside her. Like the old prophet who sacrificed a cow and built his mound around this offering, Ayak had put down a toy cow made from clay and piled mud over it. Like him she brought ash from their fire, sat in a squat, and mixed it into the mud in the basket. The baobab leaned over her, its sap moving slowly up the way energy moved up into her arms, hands. She felt herself and the tree together in that rising that was always going on. Then the moment of the full basket. Throwing it onto the mound was the motion with which a man hurled a spear. Though what was a spear? A spear made nothing last. She was building a thing of earth that would stay.

The top of the old prophet's mound had been pointed, a cone. He'd made it when the British asked men to leave their fields and cattle and build the road. But there was no pay for building the road, and when men left their fields, they endangered the harvest. The god Deng, the prophet said, showed him the place, and he sacrificed an ox there. Bring the bad things here, he said, and mix them with ash and earth and water. Throw this mud onto the mound, and when you go, the bad things will stay here.

Many came with bad things, and they brought him butter or a calf. Then they prayed and went back to their fields. But the British said the prophet had set people against the road. Their plane was metal, hard like a river rock—but the graceful marriage birds made with the air was missing. The first great noise it dropped missed the mound. The second noise lit a stand of grass, and fire burned toward the river and went out. Then the plane went away. When two years had passed, a third plane came and dropped noise, and this noise tore away the mound's height. Then the British shot the prophet and hung his body from a tree.

She mixed ash into mud and thought how Patal's stories were like laughing doves that had flown. In one story a heifer gave birth to a Dinka girl who knew how to fix disagreements between north and south, but a silver plane flew over, dropped noise, and burned up the cow that had given birth to her. She wished she were that girl born from the magic heifer. She would change her mother's mind and go to Patal's school.

The old heron woman came out of the water and watched Ayak throw a basket of mud onto the mound. The mud lodged there, glistening wet.

"You are left handed," she said, "like the old prophet. But now we have no prophets. There are only pastors. And they don't know how to cure the cattle fever."

"Pastors know paper," Ayak said.

"In this red wind," the heron woman said, "we need a prophet."

For two years since Patal's leaving, the *raau* fields languished in drought. Women ate next year's seed grain and slaughtered a cow. In the second year women gathered wild grain, and the earth priest slaughtered a cow as sacrifice, then shared the meat through the village. Now it was the third year, and the water in the baobabs was almost gone. The river's water was also small, and the herons had vanished. People no longer ate every day.

Of Akol's twenty cows nine were left. None could stand up by themselves. He got behind to hoist a cow's haunches, and Kwei took hold of its horns, and they tugged. Marial too had to be stood up. Ayak imagined one of Patal's stories suspended in an updraft the way birds hung and wheeled. Where he was there would be food.

On Easter Clarissa came from the town bringing Easter eggs and a cloth bag of *raau*. In the grain she'd nestled a small Virgin holding the dead Christ on her lap. After class Clarissa sat with Ayak beneath the baobab's obstreperous parrots. She gave Ayak a blue egg and herself one the pale pink of tamarisk blossoms.

When they peeled the eggs, both eggs were white. People too, Ayak thought, were the same inside like eggs.

Turuk skin was pink, but *Turuks* called themselves white. Northerners who had light skin called themselves green—green, they said, like an olive. The Dinka called their dark skin blue. Then *jallabah* men took Dinka women and made children, so »that now many northerners were dark as the Dinka. But northerners said Dinka were *abid*—word that meant both "black" and "slave." Did northerners not see that their own skin was the same?

Clarissa had shown her a photograph in which a pink *Turuk* man stood beside the Dinka headman. In the photo the headman's white *jallabiya* hung beneath his black face. He might walk down a Khartoum street and be taken for a *jallabah*, but when he spoke Dinka, northerners would say he was *abid*. Though neither a northerner nor a Dinka, Ayak thought, would be mistaken for a *Turuk*. In the photograph only the headman's *jallabiya* was whiter than the *Turuk* man.

A parrot flew down and pecked at the eggshells. "Why did the British want this road?"

"So that I can teach you paper and bring you Easter eggs." Clarissa smiled and leaned close. "But you don't like this road. You are sad. You feel the road has taken Patal away."

"And will the road also take you away from me?"

"I am only going to my house in town and coming back." She kissed Ayak's cheek. "It's only a path for motorcars. And who knows—Patal may return to you in a motorcar!"

But we have no motorcars, Ayak thought.

She watched Clarissa's back recede, those two ribbons dangling over her hat's brim.

Once great shouting sheets of water had poured onto the land, but now the water stored in the baobabs' trunks was gone. In the byre

Marial had lain down. Ayak lay his head in her lap. Outside the byre her mother pounded wild grain. You had to cook it a long time to take out the poison, and then it did not taste good. Ayak touched the amulet tied around her throat when her parents named her. Ayak: this name meant drought.

"Why did you give me this name 'Ayak'?"

"You were born during a dry time," Kwei said. "Now here is another."

Ayak saw how the road lay over the ground and cut off earth's breath. "Clarissa's name makes me think of a snake."

"When I was your age, northerners gave us Arabic names. I have thrown mine away."

Ayak imagined Patal's mouth making sentences and sending them across the sky, each word a stork swooping down. The only stories now flew out of Clarissa's Bible. Ayak told her mother how Christ fed whole villages with one basket of fish.

Kwei frowned. "Why does Clarissa's Christ not do this for us?"

Ayak helped Kwei carry the pounded grain to the *tukul.* She opened her science book and showed Kwei the photograph of the cell.

"A cell is so tiny we can't see it. It divides into two, and then the two divide again and go on and on dividing. Everything is made of these dividing cells. This is how things grow."

Her mother frowned. This was her daughter who knew invisible things.

"It's how your body made me," Ayak said. "A baby grows this way inside the mother, and after it comes out it keeps growing. It's how gods make the world."

Kwei's face snapped shut. "How can *Turuks* know how gods make things?"

It was as though the earth beneath their feet tore open and spread. They could see each other but could not touch. Patal and

I, she thought, are becoming paper. We go where our parents cannot go.

The river was a sliver. Crocodiles crawled onto the dry bank and died. For months Ayak had not seen a heron. Only the laughing doves and the brown parrots still ate. When the heat had lain down in dusk light, the sand grouse settled in her dirt nest. Akol returned from a village where he'd witnessed a fight between Dinka and *jallabah* soldiers.

"Afterward the soldiers loaded the Dinka's cows into lorries." Ayak followed him into the *tukul.* "You are hungry. I am sorry. And our fighters are as hungry as we are, and our land is made of distance, and they have to walk. I fear they can't come this far to help us."

"The earth priest will sacrifice a cow," Ayak said. "Then our fighters will come."

Akol pealed off his shirt and held it as though he had no weapon but this flimsy cotton.

"What is so sacred about a cow? We ourselves sell them north. We wear shirts now. You learn paper now. What is the use of a cow?"

The men had gone through *gaar*, she thought, and thought themselves warriors. Now they discovered they were only men running, falling, scrambling up, and running again. Akol let the shirt drop. From his herd of twenty only three heifers and Marial were left.

"How I wish I'd sold my cows before they died."

"Father," she said. "How was I born? Was it beneath a baobab like Patal?"

He looked as though he would like to wrap her so that the red wind could not blow in.

"It is time to tell you a difficult thing. There came a disagreement over grazing between us and some Nuer. We went there to talk. A Dinka man got angry and stuck a Nuer with his spear. We fought, and a Nuer killed a Dinka. The rest of us ran away then, but a Dinka had died, so we wanted to take something. When we passed the river, we saw your mother washing clothes. Take her child, one man said, because a Dinka was killed." He paused. "That's why you remember the mound. Your name is the name she called as I carried you off."

His eyes were like a story that hurt at the beginning but then turned bright. "I brought you to Kwei. We have only you. You have become so much ours and the village's. You with the mound inside you. You, with the blessed left hand."

The red wind hurled a spear through the air: then silence.

"I am half the dead Dinka man, half his Nuer killer."

"Do not think yourself diminished. You are not half. You are both."

"You say this because you stole. You want to pretend what you did was good."

Her father's face was a trampled place. "You have made us happy. You love us."

"Yes," she said. "And still I am like this country—I am two halves split by a road."

Heat's fields spread across the plains of wavering air. Ayak lay Marial's head in her lap. His eyes were glazed with a thin film. She thought of Clarissa's hat, its two ribbons. Clarissa came less often now, as though slowly erasing herself the way a pencil eraser took away a word.

"Ayak." Patal looked down at her. Silence hummed like a struck water jar.

He was nearly as tall as Akol. "To see you is food," she said.

"I too have waited a long time to eat."

He knelt and put his ear to Marial's belly. His smile was slow, as though he'd seen things that made him sad. He'd brought her a book in which kings wore long robes, and British soldiers made a thing called a cannon that hurled balls of metal at the *jallabahs*.

"Long ago British soldiers came to Khartoum and burned mosques. But now they give *jallabahs* planes."

He told her that in Khartoum a general had risen up with soldiers, thrown the president in prison, and declared himself Supreme Leader. Then this general moved the boundary between north and south further south. Now the oil was in the *jallabahs'* province.

"Our village owns only two guns," she said. The men had pooled cattle and traded for the first gun and kept it at the headman's house. The other gun belonged to a man who'd traded many cattle for it. "Now the men sleep in shifts."

"Both north and south have mines now," Patal said. "Our own fighters plant mines under trees where we sit for shade and think only *jallabahs* will walk there. Then these mines come loose and wash down river, and one lodges in the bank where women wash clothes. The next time the women come the mine is there."

All day the blue wind was busy weaving Patal back into the village. At dusk silence was a vast cloth holding in its threads the grass and the air. Ayak and Patal crossed the road and sat beside the mound beneath the baobab.

"I have brought back my half of the paper," Patal said.

The moon was the belly of a cow with calf. "You are fat with missionaries' food," she teased, "and I am thin. Fill me with a story."

"You are fat with teasing. So tell me. Have you asked the river god for a child?"

"The river god is not so handsome as you."

Patal lay down and pulled her down beside him. They tried the thing he called kissing.

"It's like drinking," he said.

"More like eating," she said. "Like running and then flying."

His tallness was ballast. "When we perfect this kissing, we'll show the others how."

She laughed. "We'll show them only if they pay us a cow."

She told him how Akol had stolen her.

"This is not completely a bad thing," he said. "Dinka and Nuer must learn that the sun is over both. You will teach us we are one body. You will bind us." He touched her cheek. "And I am half Dinka, half paper. Will you become the wife of a divided man? Or will you say half yes and half no?"

"I am two yeses," she said, "and no nos."

The next morning Marial was dead. That was the day the old heron woman reported the appearance of the heron at the edge of the village. It stood there, its long neck and head raised. She waited for it to fly, but it stayed. At noon she went where the men sat.

"Herons do not stand all day beside villages as though stalking people! That bird has been there since dawn, and now that bird is still warning. From that direction soldiers will come."

Patal sat with the men to decide: stay and fight, or move the village further south? He'd given Ayak coins he'd earned from the priests to buy *raau* in the town. She walked at the edge of the road where long grass brushed her legs. When the sun reached the pitch of its arc, she arrived at the town's edge. Dinka soldiers filled the road smoking cigarettes, talking. Each had a rifle slung from a shoulder strap. Though each was one man, together they seemed larger, as spots on a leopard belong to one animal. She lowered her eyes and made her way through.

At the market an old man offered her water. "Those soldiers have used up their rations. If one wants your bag of grain, he takes it. Each day they take someone's cow and roast the meat."

Soldiers, Patal had said, always eat. She looked at the map Clarissa had drawn. Would Clarissa give her sweet biscuits and tea? She turned the corner into the lane. Here was Clarissa's house—door ajar. Ayak looked in. The room was empty. A woman nearby swept her stoop.

"They were afraid of the soldiers. As we are."

In the land where Clarissa's grass was, was it rude not to say a farewell?

The fighters had gone off to their fires. She smelled meat roasting. The road rose up before her, and anger rose in her like water. On this road southern fighters had come north, and on this road *jallabah* soldiers came south. The road was half yes and half no, like the British who'd told northerners not to steal Dinka but then made a road so stealing would be easy. Half yes and half no, like Clarissa who came and went whenever she chose.

Each gust of wind was a slap. At dusk she walked with Patal to the river. The moon was the belly of a cow with calf. Where small bits of river water pooled, starlight flickered. They sat beside the mound's silence. Patal told her that the men had decided to move the village south. He began to tell a story in which Dinka stole Nuer babies and Nuer stole Dinka babies until so many babies had been exchanged that people were unable to pull apart and fight.

A shot rang out. Patal's body jolted. She heard the sound of lorries. Shouting.

Patal gripped her shoulders. "You stay here. I will come back to you."

She watched his outline dissolve in the dark. Shouts. Then a single shot loud as the crack of lightning. More shots, many at once. A woman screamed. They are killing Kwei, she thought. They are killing my father. They would kill Patal too, or take him for a slave.

She threw herself against the mound and thought of Marial. She had loved him more than her parents. It was how children loved. Now she could not be that child again. Another shout, and the smell of smoke. She lay herself, belly against the mound. It was like lying against Marial's warm side. Like lying against the side of the earth, a thing so huge it could not be moved by men.

III

On the fourth day at dusk the women and children passed beneath two flame trees into the *Turuks'* camp. Beneath canvas shades the Dinka sat crowded together. Doctors took the babies and fed them, and a fat pink man gave the women bowls of *raau* and a strange kind of milk. Ayak pushed food into her mouth and remembered the roiling smoke above the village. How thin Kwei and Nyanthon had been. Her tall father too had lost even more flesh. In the village it was not possible to have too much to eat, but in the *Turuks'* country such a thing was possible. Now the blue wind wove these pink ones into the Dinka's grass, but soon they would tear the seamless air and go back to their country. For this reason she wanted to get fat quickly.

The red wind stopped. Like an animal it had lain down. She ate and slept and woke and ate again. At night the stars came out. Every day the sun made dawn. She sat beneath the flame trees and fed her son from a bottle. The *jallabahs* who'd taken her and the other women had bound the women's eyes with cloth. One man, when he was done, pulled off the cloth and let her see his face. She'd imagined that his great grandfather must have stolen a Dinka woman, and their sons' skin was dark like the mother's. Perhaps those sons too stole women and made dark children— because now this man's skin was as black as hers. And yet he must have thought of the Dinka as slaves. Had he proved he was a *jallabah* by making her body his slave? He'd looked at her and said, "You've seen my face. Now you won't forget me. You won't forget the things I've done."

She sat beneath the flame trees watching the baby's mouth so eager to suck. You will bind us, Patal had said. He'd meant bind in a good way, by bringing the warring Nuer and Dinka together. He'd said nothing of that larger binding with the *jallabahs*. Northerners fought southerners, and the country tore, and in this tearing *jallabah* men took southern women and made babies like this boy. And those boys grew up and became *jallabah* soldiers who went south and killed their southern brothers and sisters. The road, she thought, split north from south, and it also bound north and south together. Neither northerners nor southerners liked to think about this, but it was going on.

A blossom fell, its red petals beating like a heart, and she thought of Clarissa. Clarissa had given her the beautiful mitosis. This knowledge was a thing no one could take away. Always she would know mitosis had made her, and Patal, and this baby. It had made the *jallabah*, and his father before him. Mitosis was like the blue wind: no one could step out of its weaving. She picked up the fierce red flower and held it out. The boy stopped sucking and looked at the bloom. Then he sucked again, savoring the glory of food, each swallow a looping stitch binding him to her, binding north and south together. Like me, she thought, this boy is divided. And like me, he is also someone who binds.

Slowly the days passed down into the ground. People knew the mound was inside her, and they came to her through the weaving world. She was able to see where the lost husband was, and which ones were alive, which dead. One brought her a fish he'd caught, and she put it down beside the river and began to build the mound. They knelt with her and mixed the bad things into mud and ash and threw this mud onto the mound.

When the moon rose, she stood in the light of the fire they made for her and spoke.

> *I have seen Nuer turn against Dinka, and I have seen Dinka turn against Nuer. Between us, white bones of stealing cattle. Between us, white bones of quarreling. And we fight each other over who will eat the Turuks' food. Now we are weak, and we drink Turuks' milk, but this milk has no spirit in it. Some Turuks have spirit, but their milk has no gods in it. What will they say to their children? What will they say to the children not yet born?*
>
> *We grow fat with this milk, but this milk will not give us strength. And the people of the world will not respect us until we stand up and grow our own raau. Our elders will not respect us, nor will our children. So I say to you we must live in one hut. Those around us, our skin, those we sleep beside, our breath, our bone. And we will rise with the sun and go out to the cattle and drink the milk sent down by Deng, milk which is the body of the sky.*
>
> *We will grow our own food and multiply our cattle.*
>
> *And when we have fed ourselves we will feed the northerners.*
>
> *And when we have fed the northerners, we will feed the Egyptians.*
>
> *And when we have fed the Egyptians, we will feed the Turuks. For a day will come when the Turuks will fall down on their ruined land and beg us for food.*

The fire burned down, and the people lay down on the ground. When the moon set, she lay down among them. The day after the village burned she'd walked to the *jallabahs'* camp and asked for Patal. A soldier took her to a fence made of wire with sharp points on it and left her. She stood inside the mass of heat and gripped the wire as though the force with which she held on would determine whether they let Patal go. The soldier brought him, then walked away. Patal put his hands over hers. From his mouth had come strings of words like breath beads offered to the body of air, words that had meshed her into the sighing of acacias, the glances of storks. Patal, she said, what have they done to you?

He'd looked at her and wept. He knows our parents are dead, she thought. He is too sad to speak. He opened his mouth then from which stories had flown out like laughing doves with blue powder on their wings. Some soldiers tried to find the thing that would hurt you most. Others in their instinctual stumbling chanced upon the one thing precious to you. She looked at Patal's mouth, how oddly he held it open. Then she'd seen: in his mouth there was no tongue.

Welcome to the
Torture Center, Love

I

Let me come clean. Have I paid Carbonfund $99 to offset my twenty-three-ton footprint? I have not—not yet. You think this is going to be a story. Stories have plots, you think, and plots get complicated by conflict, and you want conflict. You want conflict playing out to its satisfying end. But we don't have time for that now. We're busy stumbling around figuring out what to do. Stumbling around is not conflict. War isn't conflict either. It's more stumbling around doing real damage.

Every war has two losers, William Stafford famously said.

And they assist each other in committing suicide. Cooperative, mutual suicide is what's going on between northern and southern Sudan in '89, the year of Annie and Garang. Think flat expanse of sand, soil, weathered rock rubble—size of the United States east of the Mississippi—set with the occasional thorn tree. At the UN refugee camp near the Lol River, heat assumed the force of a bludgeon, and Michael Garang measured kids' upper forearms and performed the occasional surgery. He was having the devil's own time getting over Frances. Lush sweep of flesh she was, and he'd delivered top-drawer-quality love—and then she'd slagged him off!

He'd needed to get away. So why not pop down to Sudan, give back a little something to this country his parents fled before he was born? Docs Without Borders just the ticket, and his little humanitarian adventure gave the London hospital good press.

He was Johnny Foreigner here, though being offspring of Dinka parents, he looked utterly like the locals.

High irony, since lots of northern Arab blokes were black as the Dinka and Nuer.

For centuries Khartoum's Arabs had raided the south for black slaves and sold the Dinka and Nuer women into domestic service—including servicing their owner. And Arab males claim all offspring as heirs—if the kid's sired by me, he's automatically sterling, even if he is the issue of one of the enemy's women. So in Khartoum you saw lots of black Arabs. The president and his cabinet were dark as the Dinka. And when the president traveled to Saudi, the olive-skinned elite there gave him the cold shoulder. Add to this insult Sudan's sorry economy. Half of all kids died before age five, and the country's GNP was laughable. Which, when the president returned from Saudi, translated into shame—and shame leads to fury. Time to kick those black dogs down south—and make sure they stay kicked!

Hatred was written into the language. The Arabic word *abid* means both "black" and "slave." For this reason the Dinka and Nuer call their color blue.

A blue man then, this Michael Garang. And he was, in Dinka parlance, a *balan*. Literal meaning "expert hippo hunter," translating to women are all over him. The Médecins Sans Frontières nurses fluffed their feathers, but he gave them merely a nod. He would get Frances out of his bloody consciousness, end of story.

Late afternoon, heat backing down, he steps out of his surgery to take a look at those flame trees. Thumping aristocrats they are, planted back when missionaries roamed vastness looking for heathens. He picks up a fallen blossom, pulsing red like a floral version of the human heart, and presents it to the Dinka cutie toddling beside her mom. Moms flock to him; he speaks their lingo and holds the kids up against the sky—and is that the sound of lorries?

When the Dinka and Nuer rebel army shot down one of Khartoum's Antonovs, Khartoum forbade all flights into the south, even World Food Program grain deliveries. Hence grain must be trucked in. Now skeletal Dinka and Nuer haul in, their bones their only possessions, the compound's front gate swings open, and in come lorries. The toddler holds the red flower in one hand and with the other hangs onto Garang's pant leg, and out of the lead cab hops a rosy Renoir of a woman—slimmer than the master's models but with the soft-edged aura of *The Bathers*.

Looks like a story, feels like one, smells like one, you say. But where's the conflict? Life is not conflict. In life, events are incidental: I did this, then I did that, then they took me off the respirator. No conflict, but I'm giving you characters, and they're stumbling around fogged like the rest of us—in a place where missionaries come with a Bible in one hand and Windex in the other, as though all Africa needs is monotheism and a little economic sprucing up. The missionaries do their god thing; they build some schools and hospitals. They build roads along which franchises will eventually set up their Starbucks and Wal-Marts, and poof: Africa will disappear, and there's a mall.

I arrived the day after New Year's, Reagan's eighties winding down. Hopped down and there he was, the tallest blue-black man I'd ever seen—in surgery greens—holding in his hand a pulsing red blossom. I'd been born into the Great White Ambivalence: melt with us, but don't forget who you really are, so get out there and pick that cotton. But I wasn't having it. The darky's lamp lighting the way to whitey's front door was not cool.

"Michael Garang," he said, accent upscale Brit. He grinned. "Prime minister of the infirmary."

The southern rebel Sudanese People's Liberation Army— SPLA for short—was headed by one John Garang, a Dinka—the South's superhero, on whom depended, well, everything.

"You're related to *the* John Garang?"

"Nothing so exalted, I'm afraid. We Garangs are the Smiths and the Joneses here."

He grinned and with a mock flourish offered me the pulsing red blossom. He wore the greens and his lanky height with distinction, as though to say, "I'm Michael Garang—someone you'll want to know."

"Welcome to the Torture Center, love."

Irony, but I knew what he meant. Southern Sudan at the end of the eighties had become a killing field. Staff at the camp fed the decimated southern Dinka and Nuer and a sprinkling of other clans: all of them the northern government's victims.

"There they are, love, the starving hordes, round that baobab there, snoozing."

Baobabs are all trunk, this one so thick ten men holding hands couldn't reach around it. The branches above seem afterthought. In this dun landscape the white bark stood out. This was a great grandmother ancestor of a tree, and the Africans went there as though to refuge. They wore Western castoffs shipped in by the container load. There we were in our Hard Rock Café tees and Nikes, and there the Africans were in the tees and Nikes we'd tossed in the trash.

He pointed to the Africans' compound sectioned off from ours by chain-link.

"More skeletons napping in those *tukuls*. Note the fence between us and them, love. We UN blokes do not want our downtime littered with Third World suffering."

He shouldered my duffels and swung into tour guide patter. It hadn't rained for two years. Even the rain Dinka stored in the hollow trunks of baobabs was gone. What camp had was a borehole, and no bathing in the river, unless you wanted to host guinea worm. His parents fled during the first civil war, seventeen years of it. Now we were four years into the second.

"Thought I'd give back, since we Brits stole the store. And you?"

"I'm putting the trust fund behind me. Ditto the baked brie."

"Diamonds on the soles of your shoes, is it?"

"My daddy loves displaying his excess," I said. As though the Mercedes and Portland's hilly mansion district bordered by woods were frills I'd declined. "Owning is the drug of choice stateside," I quipped. "Then we sneak off to the toilet and throw up."

He laughed. "Sassy Annie!" he said, as though conferring a title.

I thought yes, absolutely: that's exactly who I want to be.

"Food and pay are the perks. End of perks. No train to the capital. No telly, no opera. You can read in the dining hall at night. Watch a video." He faced me. "But no strolling the countryside. It's mined. We can walk to the river, but stay on the path."

We.

I was distinctly buzzed by his vibe, which kept me from cataloguing his remarks so as to examine them later. But one stood out. When I noted his greens, he described the first time he'd watched a surgeon make the incision that exposed a beating heart.

"Heart's nothing but a pump, love. I had a laugh. Then guess what: me, sobbing like your bloody drinking fountain."

At my tent he heaved the duffels in. Then a mock flourish of a bow. Knowing he'd got my attention.

You like Garang. He's the kind women melt for. And there's the thrill of his skin and Annie's, what used to be called the race thing, and how they'll deal with that. Fine, go on liking him, but remember you're busy getting through the orange alert, emptying your carry-on of lotions and gels, while near the North Pole a chunk of ice reaches its tipping point, detaches from its glacier, and plunges hugely down into the sea.

I came from money. But senior year of high school, trying to get a handle on who I might become, I decided it was cool to eschew the material. I bought a politically correct tee—"Live Simply That Others May Simply Live"—and announced I was joining the Peace Corps. Then I changed my mind and opted for university. My first job after graduation was with World Food Program's Rome office. All this was in reaction against my father. To get away from my anorexic, invalid mom, he traveled as though the planet was Club Med, wearing privilege as though it was swanky leather the peons would naturally covet. No one took him by the back of the neck and said, "Look around you, moneybags; see what you and your kind have done."

In my mother's closet, the numbers of pairs of shoes my father gave her rivaled Imelda's. He gave her shoes as a goad—get out of bed for christsake, and take care of your daughters! But the shoes stayed in the boxes. I'd bring a pair to the bed. Wear these today, I said. And sometimes she'd put on the shoes and come downstairs. But the illusion that now she'd bake cookies and walk me to school did not materialize. She went back up, took off the shoes, and turned out the light.

When she became so emaciated that my father thought Felicia and I shouldn't see her, he carted her off to rehab. At that point I shifted my disappointment onto him: even if she was a failure, she was my mom, and my daddy was a bad man who'd taken her away—plus he lived like a pasha and gave my sister and me everything we asked for, but he had no idea how to love us. We were, I thought, abandoned children. Nor did it occur to our father that he might donate some of that excess cash to charity. He seemed to me a greedy man without generosity, and I intended to show him I was morally superior. I took the UN job with the attitude that I'd right the shocking First World/Third World imbalance by feeding starving Africans, and ignored the fact that I would pull down a very pretty salary.

My political correctness had an adolescent, self-righteous edge—but inside I was vulnerable, soft as foam, and idealistic. I wanted to put good into the world. And the job in Rome for a time had its charm—Rome with its ruins, its cuisine, its eager young men. But I was still amidst privilege so vast the populace fumbled, trying fully to exploit it. And besides, this secretarial drone was not who I was! Then, filing clippings, the photo: starved Dinka woman holding her skeletal dead kid. I stood in that office in late afternoon light and knew that I could treat my job as job and follow no flag but my own pleasure. But there was also real suffering in the world, suffering worth my attention, and I was looking right smack at it. Then this photo of the child who'd cried and cried and then stopped crying came inside me through a door I hadn't known was open.

I'll go there, I thought. I'll feed that woman. I'll go that far away.

Do you want to waste precious life time being occupied by books the way little countries get occupied by the Empire? I'm not saying don't read. I'm saying you read too much, and neglect to face the fact that melting at the poles is gathering momentum. All this reading uses up fossil fuel, and in regard to oil, reader, 'fess up.

You like driving your SUV, and you're not giving it up any time soon. You're ravenous as the Khartoum honchos. Both of you stealing the Dinka and Nuer's oil.

Tan parrots with chartreuse breasts zoomed from the acacias beside the volleyball court to the acacias next to the dining hall, and Garang squired me in. He was thirty-seven to my twenty-six, and I wondered: Would my experience stand up to his dash? We wound through jazz riffs of talk, tee logos—"Che lives!" "Viva Mitterrand!" "Put the MX on Ronnie's ranch." Docs comparing stories from their residencies. Médecins Sans Frontières nurses babbling breathy French. The fare read like a menu from El Toula in Rome: wild rice rosti with carrot and orange puree, rack of lamb with mint dumplings, banana gingerbread, amaretto macadamia cake. I chose the *cordon bleu* and chocolate mousse. So did he.

"Over here. You'll want to meet Beryl, and get a hit of her Black Label."

Think sultry salt and pepper hair, twenty years my senior and still sexy, one gold loop in her right earlobe. Beryl Scallipino was a room of smoky jazz. Her tee vintage Emma Goldman: "If I can't dance, it's not my revolution."

"I was a sixties pothead," Beryl said, "when the struggle for justice was the hottest game in town. Got stoned with thousands of other whacked out kids, then Yale law school. Started busting my ass for Tibetan janitors, Chicano bricklayers. Kept my fee scaled down, and guess what—the poorest ones made all the payments. Then came a point when the INS brick wall got me down. God was on my side, but the judge wasn't."

Loquacious mama, I thought. And will take no shit.

Staple dinner talk was the war—Khartoum's twenty million against the south's six—a war for water because, should those blacks down south divert Nile water and turn southern Sudan into

Africa's breadbasket, the northern Arabs would be up shit creek. Though the war for water paled beside the war for oil. The Dinka and Nuer had the oil, and Khartoum had a desert. Sudan was a Fourth World country, and when it broke with the Soviets, Moneybags America smelled oil, and presto the CIA was in Sudan and the Khartoum government swimming in dollars. The Khartoum honchos bought themselves BMWs and dipped into America's weapons arsenal, and once you own these shiny new toys, you want to use them. So hey, let's head south and play shoot 'em up!

In Rome I'd boned up—even hauled out my Evans-Pritchard notes from university. The Arab Baggara tribe just north of the border got paid by Khartoum to hit on the Nuer and Dinka.

"Used to be," Garang said, "that when the Baggara's cattle exhausted their grass, they said, Hey Dinka chaps, can we move our herds south? And the Dinka said, Ante up—protect us from your dastardly northern traders sleuthing for black slaves, and we'll let you onto our grass." He glanced at me. Was Annie getting it? "My Dinka relations had it off with the Baggara girls, and Baggara guys got a leg over our blue-black cuties. But now comes this war, and Baggara chaps hitting on Dinka girls say, Hey— time to marry my own kind. And Dinka chaps say, Whoops, spot of shit's hit the fan. Better get these lulus out of our sacks, or those *jallabahs* up in Khartoum will fry our asses!"

I assumed a sumptuous casualness. "Khartoum gives the Baggara guns but no salary. They raid the Dinka to feed their kids. And you can bet Khartoum's hosting their victory bash. Toasting with *merissa*, and they've butchered a cow."

He was zinged. "A bash, as you say, love, and we're not invited—we sinful devils from the West. We piss off Khartoum *and* the SPLA, strutting in our Levi's and Nikes. Reminding the locals they don't know how to settle their own affairs."

"You've got how many cousins here?" I said.

"Hundreds. And how many ran screaming from the boys with their Korans?"

"You want to grab oil land," Beryl said, "just launch a religious war. You steal oil, but that's what God wants."

Garang grinned. "What's the first question a Muslim gets asked at the door of Paradise? Tell me, the Big Guy says, how's your neighbor? Have you checked on the fellow? Sent him infrastructure? Notwithstanding that he's black, you're required to befriend the chap."

"While with the left hand," Beryl said, "Khartoum's Muslim traders haul off Dinka and Nuer and sell them around Khartoum, then Egypt, even all the way to Bonn."

"The Islamist spin," Garang said, "is that spiriting a girl north is courting. Would the lovely visit the ancestral palace for sorbet and afterward the delights of dalliance?"

"Khartoum is a hotbed of jihad," Beryl said. "And they change our money at half the going rate—half!—then use our cash to fill graves."

"Islam isn't the problem," I said. "It's the government."

"Honey," Beryl said, "in Khartoum you wouldn't even have a clitoris."

These two are good sorts, and so is Beryl, eager to spread health care and yummy eats across this guinea worm–infested world—but we don't have much time. Think about the fact that Greenland is melting! One day Greenland may just disappear. I know you work, but you could donate your car to the great Midwestern Car Dump and take a bus instead. And replace your light bulbs with the power savers. Or limit reading to daylight hours only. It matters to polar bears!

Smiling at skeletons was unsatisfactory. I needed language training. Camp's head had hired a Nuer husband and wife to run a school, and this caused a row: Why only Nuer? The Dinka and Nuer were like Arabs and Israelis but without the hardware. How they managed to agree long enough to attack Khartoum's army was beyond me. I headed to the teachers' *tukul*, mud and sticks with bits of UN turquoise tarps over the rounded top. Short, plump Nyanbol wearing a yellow kerchief waved me in.

She sat with her husband and nursed their girl, Achai Chol. "We are people together, is it not?" she said. Then she drilled me in the ritual greeting. "You have passed a good night?"

"I have passed a good night," I said. "And have you passed a good night?"

"Thank you, yes. And may God bless your day."

"May God bless your day and also this child of yours."

"And may God bless you with children and cattle."

You asked after each person, including third cousins twice removed. In no time we whipped through my sister, Felicia, and my parents.

"No grandma? No auntie? A cousin?" I shook my head. "I must feed you some relatives," Nyanbol said. "Bol and I will plump you up!"

Bol seemed designed to be her tall, slender complement. Then I saw his hands. Somewhere—and by whom?—the bones had been broken. Khartoum's torture chambers, I thought. They called those places "ghost houses." His hands had healed into blunt clubs.

"Do no worry," he said. "I can still write a pencil."

His forehead had not been scarred with the slanted cuts that meant you were one tough bull of the herd. Without this *gaar* elders considered you merely a little bull boy. But bull boys like Bol were beginning to acquire "the cattle of paper," meaning the savvy of reading and writing. They were garnering tribal elders' grudging respect.

"Your daughter," Nyanbol told him, "needs clean diaper. Please do."

"You abandoned me in London and ran away, and now you boss me," he teased, while diapering. "Why are you not kind to such a good bull boy?"

Nyanbol's laugh was sprinkling water. "It's bad to leave a husband, but I needed my grass. I came back here and said I will take this grass for my husband. So for a while I had two husbands. But now we have lost our grass."

Bol stood Achai Chol up and nudged her toward me. Her babbling was like tiny loaves of bread flung out. I lifted her and blew against her tummy.

"What's the word for your fat belly?"

"*Juny*," Nyanbol said. "Belly." Her yellow kerchief was bright, framed in the *tukul*'s doorway. She began my drill. "*Ca*: milk." Then it was on to *werj*. "*Werj*: cow."

It was crucial to own many cows. You were wealthy then, though wealth was a sidebar. The point was to hang out with cows obsessively. They were food, work, the only entertainment besides sex and dancing. Even dancing was about cows. Sex probably had a cow in it somewhere.

"I keep hearing about cows but not seeing one. I know the army rustled them. But surely there's a cow somewhere that they missed?"

"You do not need to see a cow," Nyanbol said, "but we do. In London we were bereft because without cows where is our *cieng*? Do you know this word? The blue wind weaves all things into one thing and makes the harmony of *cieng*. We found London *cieng*, but we could not find our cow *cieng*."

"We weave ourselves into cows," Bol said, "brushing against them, talking into their bodies. A man decorates his bull and struts it and sings songs in its honor, and all this is in thank-you to *cieng*."

"And learn *dheeng*," Nyanbol said. "It is your word 'dignity.' A poor man with few cattle can have *dheeng*, and a rich man with many cattle might have none. Garang, your London doctor, has *dheeng*." Her eyes turned merry. "So now learn this: when earth and sky came apart, a god appeared in this sky. And this god we called Garang. When bits of this god's power fall onto an earth man, we call that man Garang too. Many Garangs become doctors. And these Garangs are like your London one. They make us laugh."

Before I left I wanted to kiss Bol's hands, but refrained. Nyanbol, I thought, must have kissed those hands many times.

What we've got here, people, is an actual sun god—to the hundredth power. It pulls you in, makes you want to keep reading. Everybody loves a sun god, everybody wants one of their own, and look: a Kenyan cook takes up with a New Hampshire doc, a Nuer security guard with an MSF nurse. People are getting it on. Garang is a Dinka, and for Dinka flirting is an art you'd better be damn good at. He likes to flirt, plus it will give Annie time to get used to Refugee Hell.

The heat moved slowly, like a grinding stone, I thought, turned by oxen. Imagine a place of drought far from any town. Crops and wild plants dead. John Garang's hungry soldiers trek the barren waste on foot, pass the skeletons of cows, come upon a village. They find one scrawny cow, butcher it for the evening meal. Next morning they claim the villagers' seed grain, saved for next year's planting, and trek on. Women pick leaves from the few trees and boil them. They bind their stomachs and the stomachs of their children to staunch their hunger. Here and in the surrounding villages two hundred Dinka die each day. There are no kids under the age of two left alive.

Those in the villages who were strong enough to walk begin to walk toward the UN camp. Just after dawn another bevy of mothers with kids dragged through the gate. Old men hobbled, poling themselves with walking sticks. A daughter carried her bone-dangle mother in her arms. Through the morning they poured past those flame trees flanking the gate as though down a sluice. They were the evidence that whole villages had burned. They sat, blocks of dark salt.

"They'll beg for your sunglasses, watch, camera," Beryl said. Her gold earring gleamed. "But don't give gifts. You don't know their clan, other clans will be pissed, and rivalries are murderous—plus everyone feels confined and bored out of their minds."

We sat side by side and dished out red sorghum the Africans called "Reagan *raau*." Dinka men said, Eat Reagan *raau*, and you could fuck all the way to morning. This mythologized the powerful West, but what did I know?—I wasn't eating *raau*.

A problem right away was that I could not quickly make the starved better. I told myself that these people in the feeding lines were gaining, it was happening. Then I'd see the flies around the babies' mucous eyes, and a skeleton supported on either side by two other skeletons faltering toward the infirmary. Their cattle, *tukuls*, pots, gourds, blankets had disappeared. Their cousins, uncles, elders had disappeared. They themselves were disappearing, flesh evaporating like sweat in the heat.

Mid-morning Garang strolled over. "Let's hear it for this great fundamentalist republic!" he said. "They keep these skeletons coming!" He meant to amuse. Loosening the social fabric, he called it.

"A little street theater for the populace?" I said.

"Checking on your welfare, ladies. Making sure you're enjoying every comfort." He addressed the refugees through a mock megaphone. "Be of good cheer, friends! We shall not overfeed you!"

"Some speak English," Beryl said, "though they might not pick up on the irony."

He ignored this. "I say, ladies: no one's leaving. Guess they like the food."

Those legs of his had to be the longest, lankiest in Sudan.

"Sassy Annie." He leaned down, lips near my ear. "At least let me smell your perfume. I get very few perks." Then he straightened. "Do I have your blessing?"

"We're not knitting any socks," I said.

I watched him walk back across the compound and into the infirmary.

"He digs your Catherine Deneuve mouth," Beryl said. "And there was a remark to the effect that 'she assumes the mantle of her eroticism with élan.'"

"He's a mensch, obviously. How come you're not with someone?"

"No one's lifting my lid. My sweetie died, melanoma at thirty-two. Boom, gone. Also guys in aid work lack flirting skills. They've watched too much porn."

I saw Garang and two nurses head toward the front gate. A squadron of parrots screeched across the compound from one stand of acacias to another, and he knelt and waved me over. On the ground lay a woman in a green plaid dress flanked by two men. One man wore a sarong tied at the waist. The other was naked. Their skin had lost its cast and turned smoky. The men's eyes darting, exhausted.

When you've crossed the Rubicon and there's no going back, swelling sets in. The men's feet were blunt clubs. The woman's swelling had already progressed upward. Her torso was bloated, the green plaid across her belly unbuttoned. Her face distended. Eyes slits. My first impulse was Self-Righteous Overwrought: this is outrage not to be borne, and we *Turuks* will put a stop to it. It was a stock stance. I had a flash then that it might become difficult to maintain stock stances in Africa. Garang took the woman's hand. She inhaled. Then her breath turned and went out.

"Gave them morph," he said. "All we can do."

Parrots made a raucous dash across the air—life goes on!

I was fielding lust and affection—he was so damn charming, and he had an easy dignity and this thing we call humanity, which among horny men is often in short supply. Garang did the tender thing then. He closed the woman's eyelids. Imagine the hundred thousand flakes of skin a minute falling from our bodies, mingling with motes in the air, becoming dust. We looked at each other and knew that whatever might happen between us, this mesh of moments would be our bedrock.

Scientists shout: we humans are the enemy at the gates! And what do we do? We go right out and buy SUVs. The Sahara was held in place by a thin crust of lichen and tiny stones. Then bye-bye, camels; yo, vehicles. Wheels churned and still churn away this delicate cover, and storms sweep that dust as far as the Arctic—where it darkens the ice and makes it melt faster. Now the Sahara is moving south, people, invading southern Sudan's Sahel, and the lush bread basket of the Sahel will also disappear. Sudan, both north and south, is drought—and war—courtesy of gringos' rapacious goodwill. A war of the armed against the defenseless, and the bottom line is food. In the south there isn't any.

After dinner the brown parrots with chartreuse breasts sat in the acacias beside the dining hall and surveyed all who exited with critical appraisal.

"Stroll to the river, love? Pretend we're in Kew Gardens."

Single file on the path—the land might be mined—so I went first. At the far edge of the tarmac, four hyenas, round ears in silhouette.

"These gals live in female clans—you should like that: a pack of feminists. Two cubs, at most three, and the cubs play, and eventually one cub kills the other two."

"You're making this up."

"True every word. Bloody ballsy, these dames."

I was jazzed on Garang ogling my ass, and then I saw the tamarisks, which signal water, and there was the Lol—all that wetness rushing toward the Nile, then on to Egypt. Garang picked a tamarisk sprig and examined its pink fuzz of blossoms. He pointed downstream: a crested crane in the shallows. Above a long lavender neck the crane's head was black with white and red stripes. The spiky crown like long, shimmering hat pins thrust into a pincushion.

"That this crested chap's here at all is thanks to Brits."

I gave him a playful nudge with my shoulder. "Only evolution can make a crested crane."

"Cranes are tasty, love, and if we Brits hadn't insisted on the permit, he'd be gone like the elephants. One animal per year—and you had to take it with spears, arrows, snares. No guns allowed; that should please you. Then we Brits pulled out, and Khartoum's General Hammad came with helicopters. Scuppered twenty-five elephants a day. Though now humans are the Hammads. We humans are not an endangered species, love. We're the plague."

"It's Garang's BBC World Service live," I teased.

"BBC is what I do in lieu of getting smoochy kisses."

"One of the nurses might give you a whirl," I said, "if you weren't continuously occupied with polishing those boots of yours."

"On the contrary, love, vanity is your bailiwick. I wouldn't think of intruding."

"Who actually irons his greens—irons!—in the desert!"

He grinned, then turned serious. "Tell me everything I need to know."

Suddenly I wasn't Sassy Annie. I was the girl whose mom had starved herself.

"My father got an MBA, then determined to live as though he'd come from money. When he entertains, he hires string quartets and uses food to show off. The food's his way of getting in my anorexic mom's face. Once I asked what she was like before they married. She ate, he said.

"Once I made two cucumber sandwiches the size of silver dollars—bread, slice of cuke—no butter, no mayo—on a blue willow plate. I carried it up to her room, but she would eat only one. So I ate the other. I told myself we were actually dining together."

Garang handed me the tamarisk twig. "Pink Cloud Tamarisk Annie. I didn't know what it was. It made me want to protect you."

His long legs folded up like a chaise, and he pulled me down beside him. I flipped my mother's ring on its chain from beneath my tee.

"Her wedding ring." I thought of the housekeepers who'd let Felicia and me jump on beds, who gave us snacks whenever we asked. "My little sister saved me. I got good vibes feeding her, and I was determined that she and I would flourish. Now you."

"My folks fled to London, and bingo I was born. Had my electric train flanked by sheep and hedgerows—but they also steeped me in cattle songs. Weekends our house filled with women cooking, men talking Parliament, candidates. But school was hard. I'd be high on soccer, white boys' skins and mine open under the sun—and some kid would hit me with 'Nig!'" He paused. "My golden retriever, Majok, was my chum."

The heat was backing down. We watched the river purl along.

"You heard of that chap who strung his tightrope over your Niagara Falls? He took along a stove and in the middle cooked an egg. That's me, love—scrambled egg on the cusp." He grinned. "But don't forget, I come from privilege. My father's lecturers levered him into a prestigious firm. We hung out with the pale upper crust: that's how I got into Cambridge. I'm whiter than you, love—save for my skin."

That moment felt like a pivot: it was time to play. "Take off those shiny boots, Garang. Let's see you get down and dirty."

"Is this a come-on, this invitation to undress? What will I get for it?"

"The feel of your very own African mud between those spiffy Brit toes."

He laughed, then knelt, and picked a vine's fruit.

"*Kwol-jok*. Wild cucumber. If you get sick, love, I slice the sacred cuke in half. Fling the halves up. If they land open side up, you'll live."

"And if both halves fall face down?"

"Means you're scuppered. But I throw them up again. I toss cukes into the air until I bring 'round the result I want."

"Gods change their minds?" I said.

"On the head. The immortals can be nudged."

Walking back in the dark was foreplay. At my tent he paused.

"You look very fetching. And should you continue to provoke, I cannot be responsible for the consequences."

"And what, pray tell, might those be?"

A beat, the way an actor pauses for emphasis. "Are you testing my waters?"

"Just with a toe."

"I blather about getting a leg over. But I don't want to rush us headlong."

I looked up. "All this Dinka height makes your mouth seem very far away."

"I'll lie down!" he said.

"Yes," I said. "Do that."

———

You're reading when you could be paying farmers in Jamestown, Rhode Island, to delay haying their fields until after birds have completed nesting—

"That was Christmas for rock stars," he said next morning. "Look what I have."

"You certainly had me." I kissed his nose. Those parents from a village near Abeyei had risen. He was upper crust, flamboyantly. Precisely because he had Cambridge credentials he could say, "In Khartoum I'd be lucky to be a doorman at the Acropole Hotel."

"You need to know I'm Type A," he said. "I hope to ease out of that some."

"You don't dawdle. You need to learn dawdling."

"But if I dawdle, the world might collapse! And you, Tamarisk, might disappear."

I flashed on the refugees waking in their *tukuls*, others on their way to the camp.

"It's the skeletons who are disappearing."

He turned wistful then. "We're matey, you and I. You know that, don't you? Me the black dude trying to measure up. You with your hungry heart wanting to feed the starving. We signed on to ease the world's pain. That's the glue that sticks us together."

"Why do you want a paleface?"

"Because it drives white boys crazy," he teased. "Though I look at your Yank bod and think, This woman was born in that skin, and I've had to scramble." His eyes turned impish. "Then I get condescending. Those clueless U.S. types, I think, they seem a bit stupid." He kissed my ear. "You'll want to know about my first affair—with SAR11. Don't laugh—they're microscopic chaps of the oceans. More of them than any other creature. This bloke comes on the telly, says they're teeny and so bloody many that they'll never go extinct. So I took up with the chaps. When things went bad at school, SAR11s cheered me on." He raised a fist. "We die, individual SAR11s die—but the great horde of SAR11 goes on!"

"SAR11 solidarity forever!" I said.

He sat up. "So listen, Tamarisk. Do you accept me as your obsessed?"

"Be my obsessed."

"Is there a bloke in the wings? Because I'd have to challenge him to a duel."

"No bloke."

"I can be the bloke, then? I feel I'm about to say ridiculous things."

"You already have, darling." Darling. I was signing on.

The immortals can be nudged. You put up with my preaching, so I gave you some scenes. Now I'll give you this—these lovers come to the sweltering bush, the universe delivers them each other, and in the cauldron of southern Sudan, what more could they want? But people swear to love and don't imagine the conditions in which they won't be able to keep the vow. These two imagine the swath of time out ahead, how they'll take it by handfuls, and have no way of knowing how little time there will be.

II

Imagine heat in slow amble across the compound. The brown parrots fluff their chartreuse breasts and dine on insects. I was getting used to my new status as Garang's woman the way you get used to a dress you'd previously thought too risqué.

I intended to bask. But how bask in Hell? Feeding refugees was like pouring water into a river: What difference was it making? It was tossing an elephant an after-dinner mint.

Two Africans dragged through the gate, one in a shirt with one sleeve ripped away. He'd used the sleeve to bandage his friend's head. A nurse took the bandaged one to the infirmary. I gave the other a bowl of *raau*. I remember looking at the torn shirt, his bare arm. Maybe there were no sores on his arms then, or maybe there were a few and none of us caught them, the warning signs of *kala-azar*, which gets so painful that at the end you go mad.

Monyluak was his name, and he'd learned English in a missionary school. He ate fast. Then a tear slid down his cheek. Northern soldiers had burned his village and taken the survivors in lorries. He and his friend with the bandaged head managed to run away. They walked five days, no food. At the river, other Dinka were waiting. A boat came: traders who'd brought guns south and were taking ivory north. The Dinka got on the boat. Later some SPLA attacked the boat for the ivory, the traders shot at the SPLA, and in confusion—or on purpose?—the traders began to shoot the Dinka.

"We jumped in the river. I could not count how many went beneath. After that my friend and I walked many days. Each morning I saw the sky, and a small knife entered my heart—the knife of sweet life."

When he was eight, his parents, who'd lived by selling firewood, died. A trader captured him, but he slipped away. Later a potter taught him to make bowls, and when he was eighteen, a woman bought one and befriended him.

"That man who came with me is her husband," Monyluak said. "The day the soldiers burned our village they did bad things to women. When they took my friend's wife, he shouted and broke away. Two soldiers held him, and another soldier cut off his ear. That soldier laid the ear in my hand. Keep this for your friend, he said. So he cannot say we took anything from him."

Monyluak reached inside his shirt and brought forth a small bundle. He unfolded the cloth as though to reveal an emerald. The ear was shriveled, like something ancient stolen from the dead.

The ice warms and dribbles, the Sahara crumbles, and in Cairo a blinding sandstorm with high winds fans a small fire into a holocaust. Gringos want oil, Khartoum wants oil, the Dinka and Nuer want oil, Larry McBride of Chevron wants oil, and the right hand too wants oil—though the left hand is smarter, wider, deeper, less subject to appetite, more given to tears. It's because of the right hand's lust for oil that Monyluak paces the volleyball court weeping, his hands clasping each other as though they have no other hands to hold.

Monyluak was there every day like a monk carrying a bowl that brims with pain. He was there pacing at dusk when Larry McBride rolled in. Think blond, hulking *Turuk* fed on steak and milk, a Kirk Douglas jaw. He hopped down, stack of white tees over his arm, CHEVRON in red lettering above the stars and stripes.

I found Beryl hanging her wet panties on the line. She took a clothespin from her mouth. "Born with a double espresso in his veins. Marsden will pee his pants."

Marsden, the camp's head, had a blond ponytail. He was lean, plain, disciplined, and fond of quoting Gandhi. We'd teased him about not lifting a glass—that's why the UN sent you to this desert: you failed the whiskey exam. Larry wasn't the sort Marsden cultivated, Beryl said, but no matter. Larry had cultivated Marsden. He'd tooled into camp one day with a bottle of Chevron Scotch, brought his espresso machine into the office, plugged it in, and brewed them both a cup. Marsden didn't drink Scotch or espresso. No matter. Larry did. The refugees were a damn shame, and it was good to see folks getting the problem squared away. He was up the road, and the crew here should come take a look. They had air conditioning and a pool flanked by palms airlifted from the coast. The Sudan Hilton transported to scrub, but crews needed perks. After all, they were getting the Africans' oil out of the ground for them. Joint ventures the humane way to render the Third World competitive. Let's give these people a boost—pump their oil, and we both profit!

Larry peeled off a tee for each guard at the gate, then doled out tees to passing refugees. Marsden stepped from his office. Think the sixties without drugs.

"Checking out the sediment around here?" Marsden said.

"Yup. See can we help these people out. Talked my way through the checkpoints. And crossed a few palms. Money talks, and here it really talks."

"You're south of the border," Beryl said. "Working for the SPLA now?"

He laughed. "Would if they'd hire me. Funny thing about oil. Everybody wants some. Me, I'm the oil witch. I can smell it. Smells like lions in rut."

Marsden had a pinched look. "You'll join us for dinner?"

"Don't mind if I do. Stay the night with you good people." Larry handed me a tee and slapped one against Marsden's belly. "I'll get us some Chevron Scotch from my rig."

With Larry you couldn't say no. Marsden went along to the Land Rover.

"He looks harmless," Beryl said. "But getting the Dinkas' oil out of the ground means delivering it to the mullahs. Larry makes bucks and helps genocide along."

"But you love to watch him get under Marsden's skin?"

Beryl laughed. "You got it."

Larry's another gringo doing the dollar sign thing. The biz man is a stock type like those pink plastic flamingos in trailer parks. Very soon you want him to go away. Meanwhile a snowcapped volcano in southern Colombia, dormant for five hundred years, erupts with great force. And in similar fashion, without a shred of conflict, one species after another dashes to the cliff and over the edge. Meanwhile commerce and corruption stroll confidently on, and the earth's oil dwindles. So don't just trade in your SUV for a Prius. Start taking the bus when you're in a hurry, and when you've got some margin, start walking. Walking is generally good for animals, so get into your animality; notice it feels good to be outside hearing birds chirp, seeing leaves fluffed by breeze, sniffing the smell of the live earth—it's not made of asphalt and steel! And guess what: the research is in that people are generally happier when they're around dirt. Why do you think people go nuts every spring planting gardens, filling flower pots, buying rose bushes?

After Beryl and I bathed, she went off to drink Scotch with Larry, and a weepy MSF nurse told me the latest story about three hundred Dinka in Abeyei boarding a train to Khartoum. I was blown open. You hear one of those stories, and you think, I can't manage this: the knowledge that some people actually did this to some other people. I needed Garang. The parrots had perched in the acacias. Smell of oregano: pasta night. Garang was reading in the video room, giving each sentence his piercing attention. I stepped in bearing the train story like the head of John the Baptist on that platter.

"Tamarisk! Listen a mo." He was revved. "Newton's passed the sell-by date, and now that chap Heisenberg pops down with his Uncertainty Principle. Says you can't see a thing objectively because your looking influences the thing you look at. In effect you're a slice of what you're looking at—though the fellow doesn't say exactly that.

"Then some other chaps put it about that what happens in one spot affects what happens in other spots. This event right here knows right away what's going on far away, and immediately gets in step. The orchestra stays synced." He stabbed the page with his finger. "Then they come out with the really big one. This business of events knowing about other events happens at the subatomic level. *And* it also happens at our big, blundering level of trams and trips to the theater and my kissing you up one side and down the other. What it means, love, is we are so connected that there is *no way* to come apart. Is this not top drawer!?"

"Does this mean I can't lose you?"

He watched my smile go haywire. "Tamarisk? Something's hurt you."

"Three hundred Dinka in Abeyei," I said, "boarded a train to Khartoum."

Some grain got shipped by rail, and Dinka rode the empty cars back north. Grain going south to feed the starving, and the starving fleeing north because they had no grain. Never mind that in Khartoum they would live in Hillat Kusha, that slum built on a toxic dump. It would be safer there than here because here was not safe.

Soldiers helped them into the cars. Soldiers slid shut the doors. The train began to move. Some of the Dinka were weary and lay down. Mothers nursed their babies. Children started a singing game. In the next car more children took up this song. It felt good to hear singing, and the thrum and clack of wheel on track was music taking them to a safe place. That sound and the motion lulled them. Then the train slowed. Stopped. No window through which to look out. They heard a man's voice shouting Arabic. Then the sound of splashing against the outside of the cars. And fumes. A man shouted the word: petrol! A baby, in surprise, let go of the mother's nipple. The sound of splashing stopped. A woman began to weep. How long did her voice go into the air like a monk going down a street begging food? There came another sound like many whips, flaying the air. Someone began to sing. Others took up the song. For a while the sound of singing drowned out that other sound. Then that other sound rose and drowned out the singing.

These two are in the midst of a killing famine, and war stories are a notorious turn-on. The closer and the more heated the slaughter, and the more hungry and skeletal the Africans are, the more soldiers, aid workers, and refugees fuck. It's *carpe* the *diem*, life is not a dress rehearsal, get it while you can, time's winged chariot—and now add to the mélange that dwindling oil, that melting ice.

The train story was peyote. Garang and I went into the dining hall with every window of every cell wide open. Others were dead, horribly, but we were alive.

Swan, as we called her, was an MSF nurse slim as a tendril twinning up a column. Black curls framed a face so pale you imagined her twirling a parasol. Even as a baby, she'd said, my neck was long, so they named me Cygne. She was Catholic and subsisted on sparing portions. I'd never seen her drink a Coke, let alone a UN smoothie. Garang had scrubbed his laundry and teased her. How much to do mine, Swan? Name your price.

If I do your wash, I will not charge.

No charge! Swan, I could use a wife like you. What say we marry up?

She'd smiled. My father will say no, she said. Because you have no cattle.

It was her birthday, so the cooks got fancy with hors d' oeuvres. Cans of caviar from that original airlift, smoked salmon.

"Our French miss here's not chowing down," Larry said.

"Swan," Beryl said, "you look like you came from a concentration camp."

"I came out of *malheur*," Swan said. "For *le petit déjeuner* just coffee. At night, never fish. Only bits of lamb for the *gigot*. The butcher my mother worked for gave it." She ducked her head, then smiled at Marsden. "Now I am vegetarian like you."

Marsden blushed but was saved by a cook presenting Swan's birthday cake. We belted out "Happy Birthday," offered her little presents.

"Think of cake as communion wafer," Beryl said. "You're ingesting the body of Christ, Swan. Isn't that what you Catholics say? It's very Catholic, eating chocolate."

"I too have present to give," Swan said. From beneath the table she produced a man's shirt—still folded and pinned. Ocean blue with motif of green palm trees and yellow streaks of flitting fish. "I see the fish and think of Christ's disciples. They catch fish in nets; then Christ makes these fish many. He feeds big crowd." She looked at Marsden. "You are this same. You give from your salary to Africans. So I want to give you this Christ shirt."

"Me?" Girls had not fantasized the wetness of his kisses.

"Take out pins, please," Swan said. "I want to see it fit to you."

He obliged, a giant made clumsy by being observed. Beryl was caustic.

"No longer do you look like a Mennonite with a buggy parked out front."

"Well, thanks," Marsden said. He flushed and to cover embarrassment changed the subject. "Now if our grain shipment would arrive, I'd be set."

"These Arab types don't move," Larry said, "except you fire off a hydrogen bomb. Only other way is moolah for the mullahs. Get that milk cow the UN to fork over a hefty bribe, and you'll get your grain. And don't forget the rail car shipment parked up at Babanusa. Just waiting for your claim check."

"The Phantom Shipment," Beryl said. "Baba's a garrison town, for heaven's sake. You think the general in charge is politely holding our grain until we mosey up there instead of selling it himself?"

"Marsden's UN man in Khartoum said it arrived," Larry said. "So I heard."

"Marsden, my man," Garang said, "we'll seize the day, you and I, pop up to Baba! You with the Arabic, me with Dinka." He mimed a hug. "We're perfect for each other."

"Oh give me a break," Beryl said. "You two just want to tool the countryside."

These two lovers haven't had a single argument. They are the privileged. They suffer only the bites of mosquitoes, the occasional indigestion from overeating. In the end they'll eat pot roast, fuck each other's eyes out, then die, first one, then the other. Meanwhile mallards by the thousands die in Idaho, the seas float zillions of genes we didn't know existed because human eyes can't see their wavelength of light, but an excess of small plastic pellets called Mermaid's Tears dumped in the oceans are taking these genes down.

And the ice has gotta do what it's gotta do.

So get going! You could start by trashing your Humvee, getting off the Stairmaster, and walking to work! And get on those congresspersons! Congresspersons must be prodded, and who will do this? You think someone else will do it for you?

We stood outside beneath the moon, passing a joint. People started peeling off, and Garang and I headed to our tent. I lit the hurricane lamp.

"I could pour gin in a drip," he said, "all from imagining the slope of your thigh."

"Not you, darling. You're a Cambridge-certified doc, and you don't make mistakes." He nibbled my shoulder. We helped each other undress. "Eat me."

"Oh but Tamarisk—Dinka man dare not be greedy. It's bad form."

"You're a Brit, darling. Brits are gorgers, and aggressive."

"Let me be a gorger, then." He slid down and began kissing the inside of my thigh. He was silent only when he did surgery— and this. I got into heavy breathing.

"I'm performing splendidly, it seems," he said.

"You are vain. And tomorrow you'll polish your boots, as though this is London."

"Nature of Dinka man, love. Your lip gloss don't hold a candle. I decorate my ox with bells, and off we prance, me looking sharp with my dazzling spears."

"I'll watch your ox go by, and you'll make me your first wife."

"I'll make you my one wife. Brits don't keep stables."

"And what have we got in common besides sex, in your sweet opinion?"

He rose on one elbow. "Are we not idealists of the first order? You with your heart stuck open, me with my penchant for stitching up gashes."

He sat up and affected taking my pulse. "Methodical, your heart, Tamarisk. Your pulse is doggedly steady. Exactly what we want: a bloody mailman of a pulse." He paused. "I must also take your other pulse, the femoral one." His free hand touched that place where the inside of my thigh met torso. "By taking both pulses at once, I can know if you have coarctation of the aorta. Rare, but it will kill you." He listened with his fingers. "Lucky woman. I pronounce you free of this malady."

"You want to touch me there. You fabricated this excuse."

"Coarctation is no fabrication. Though I confess I do want to touch you in these two places. One hand on the north pole, one on the south. I've got the whole world in my hands." He affected deep listening. "What's this? Sailing down your river a great boatload of cheeky chutzpah! And—uh oh!—here comes flirting and promiscuity. I'll have to keep an eye on you!"

Suddenly I was sobbing. "That train," I said.

He embraced me, coils of comforting.

"I can't stand the world going so haywire," I said, sobbing. "I know people suffer all around this damn world—but they're your people!"

I sobbed. He kept holding me, kissing me with little kisses. He dropped his flashy I'm So Smart And Charming mode and got basic.

"I know, Tamarisk. I know."

He said it the way a mother says to her baby, Mommy's right here, don't worry sweetie, we're hurting together, but it's going to be better soon. He kept holding me, letting me be sad. He had patience. He *had* to have patience. It was what happened to you if you weren't a white-skinned gringo.

He kept holding me, and we drifted in the long boat of quiet. He'd tossed down his Levi's—garment that sheathed his long legs and that later I'd invest with religious significance. I glanced at the Levi's in hurricane lamplight. The suffering around us would go on, I thought. But I also imagined we were going to live forever.

No one in southern Sudan should get used to the sound of lorries at night. These two will think many times about that night, those men. Were those who came Khartoum's soldiers wanting to make a buck reselling humanitarian grain? Or the south's SPLA away from base camp needing to provision themselves? Or Baggara Arabs just north of the border cadging food for their families because Khartoum gave them guns but no cash? Whoever they were, they must have congratulated themselves for lifting a little something from the pink gringos who could well afford to part with it.

When the crew woke the next morning, they found the guards bound and gagged. And the doors of the warehouse thrown open. And the warehouse empty. And the grain gone.

III

The morning after the break-in Larry tooled out of camp before dawn. Garang and I came to breakfast looking smoochy. You two neck it up, a doc said, and I can't get a single frog in my sack.

Marsden had told me his parents lived on a commune, and when he was seven, a girl playmate took him along fishing. A trout hit her line, she landed it, and he saw the hook in the corner of its mouth. I watched it leap against the pain, he'd said, and that was the end for me. No more eating animals. Now he announced the break-in and blushed. He'd been caught short.

"A break-in?" a doc said. "Call the fuzz!"

"The fuzz," Beryl said, "may be the culprits." She meant Khartoum's General Adide, who had orders to see to our welfare, but he was a hundred miles south in Wau, and it might have been his soldiers who'd copped our grain.

"Could have been Adide's army," Marsden said, "or the north's Baggara Arabs. Or even SPLA. Sounds crude, SPLA stealing food from Dinka and Nuer they're fighting for, but it happens. Soldiers always eat."

Staff's food wasn't kept in the grain warehouse but upstairs above the dining hall. "Our stores weren't touched," Marsden said. "But there's nothing for Africans."

"Radio Wau," Beryl said. "Summon the general up for a tour of our warehouse and ask him to bring along a load of grain."

Marsden flushed. "You think a general's going to drop by for a Coke?"

She flourished the hair. Let Marsden sulk in his miserable little carapace of a body, where no one ate, drank, or pissed. *She* had a body, and it was glory!

News has become mere anecdote: one person crowned Miss America, another beheaded. It's mostly image now, and here I am with the *Times* in one hand, a latte in the other, and on page one what we've got is another bloody Iraqi mom in Fallujah flinging herself onto the body of her third dead son. Is the blood hers, his, or both? We had some dead sons in 9/11, and I remember the face of one mom: her son's smoke. Sorrow comes and goes, but it comes again, and keeps coming, and at some point you're an old mom, and here it still comes. We went bananas after 9/11, revved up our production line, and started turning out more dead sons. Our dead sons, their dead sons, this is turning into a trillion-dollar markup—and it makes melting worse.

Yes! I told you we don't have much time—and have you noticed how your right hand doesn't know what its twin is doing? Tear yourself away from your nightly bowl of Netflix, and observe your right and left hands.

Brown parrots with pale chartreuse breasts flapped over Mony-luak pacing the volleyball court. In our tent Garang affected casualness.

"Marsden wants me to pop up to Baba with him. Chase up those rail cars of grain so we can feed the locals."

"You're going on some crazed jeep ride through the war zone?"

The road from here to Baba was Khartoum's territory. The SPLA dashed in, hit and run, and the *murahaleen*. And the random hungry man with a gun. There was a saying: You're trash without a Kalashnikov. Get some cash with a Kalashnikov.

"It's safer with double the blokes," he said. "Wouldn't you agree?"

Crisis was mine. "Darling, I'll go. Marsden and I are whiteys."

"I would like you to keep your delectable white self ensconced behind chain-link." He tried for lightness. "I'm your elder, Tamarisk. Think a day, two at most."

"But you're a Brit. Suppose you run into SPLA, and they find out that you're someone they could hold for ransom? And if you run into Khartoum's army? You look like one of the million blacks who won't go away."

"I speak the lingo here," he said. "I can't let Marsden down."

"This is so damned male of both of you! You don't even know if the grain's in those cars. And I'm supposed to stay put and weave a tapestry?"

He was amused. "And what exactly is it you ladies would do?"

"We wouldn't send you." I lay my forehead against his chest.

"I can't scupper Marsden," he said. "And he's absolutely not taking a woman out there." He kissed my cheek. "Am I not forging out, battling the elements and sundry cyclopes and dragons— all to bring you back the Holy Grail?"

"So it's slam bam thank you ma'am?"

He burst out laughing. "I will disprove that in short order." He stood back and assayed me. "I'd envisioned composing a rather more elaborate speech to win you, love, but here we are. Sassy Annie, Pink Cloud Tamarisk, will you have me as your husband?"

I zinged: this was The Gold. I lifted the chain over my head: my mother's ring. I'd never taken the ring off. Now I reached on tiptoe and laid the chain around his neck.

"Pray this damn government doesn't make me a widow first."

I do a quick overview of the *Times* for balance. Here are two stories, section D, side by side. AIDS flourishes in Africa, but on the facing page we donate surplus wheelchairs to challenged Tibetan orphans. It looks like balance at first, but both stories are about damage. Damage is not balance. Some of us out here are balance junkies, and I don't see myself getting off this without some pricey intervention. Let's see some actual Good toe-to-toe with Evil!

Oh but wait—page 45: dolphins. And not just dolphins cavorting. This is dolphins saving frail humans from a shark attack. Dolphins surround the swimmers—for forty minutes!—holding off starving sharks. But is it legit to starve sharks? Jesus would say no. Ditto Peter Singer. I see where this is leading. It's leading to a law requiring swimmers to carry shark rations at all times—or some other attempt to get it right. But have you noticed that when we decide to make things better, we may just as easily make things worse? This is a tough one, and the right and left hands had better negotiate in good faith—otherwise the talks will collapse.

At the checkpoint outside Babanusa Marsden shook him awake. Beside the hulk of the bunker, soldiers stood in the heat, each with his Kalashnikov, his allotment of boredom. Sorry chaps, he thought, sentenced to the company of other men, also bored. The lieutenant requested papers. They had no pass, but Marsden's Arabic was fluent.

"Wave your black bag," Marsden said.

The lieutenant signaled them through. "Cribbage!" Garang said.

It was the dusk hour when the color of the light changes. They passed tight rows of mud and concrete houses. Women prepared the evening meal. A child walked beside a thin dog. Arab country, and the north's squaddies. Any Dinka here were refugees. Blokes huddled under that baobab, he thought, look like me. And here it was: the rail station. From when Brits policed the countryside collecting taxes for themselves and Egyptians. Brits were gone, but their brass hinges and Doric columns remained. Stile, stanchion, strut—blunt announcement of their clout. The office was shut. They went around back.

"Well, will you look at that?" Garang said. On a spur at the back of the yard, nine cars. Weeds growing beneath them. He whistled. "Precisely as Larry described."

"The guy drives me nuts," Marsden said. "But he's the best source I've got." They crossed the yard, shook the cars' locks. "Let's head for the brigadier."

They drove toward the center of town. Streets crowded, jostling, the market bustling. *Jallabahs* in long white robes sharing a smoke.

"See the two Dinka moms," Marsden said, "talking to that *jallabiya* who's got their boys by the hand?" The boys looked to be eight, nine. Now the robe hustled them along, turned them down a side street. One boy wrenched round to look back, eyes like white handkerchiefs waving. Garang flung open the door, leaped down, pressed through the crowd. When he reached the side street, the three had vanished. Women in doorways stared at him: black man in safari suit? What had he imagined he'd do—slam the robe upside the head? His sprint had drawn a crowd. He headed back, climbed in.

"Bloody wankers!"

"Only young girls bring a higher price than those boys. And the moms figure that way the kids will eat."

"That was not a smart move I just did. Put a hold on me, will you?"

Marsden produced one of his rationed smiles. "Fat chance, stopping you."

At the market entrance a man in a white *jallabiya* flagged them. Wiry, sinewed—and dark as any Dinka. He thrust his hand through Marsden's window: shake. They went back and forth in Arabic.

"We're invited to tea," Marsden said. "He's a trader, probably. Or a spy working for the brigadier. Or both. I told him about the break-in. Played up our plight."

They got down. Call the chap Mr. Fix-It, Garang thought. Bloke barked a command, and tea was brought out to the road. Much attention on Marsden's blue shirt bright with yellow fish, Garang's safari suit. Fix-It dispatched a man to the brigadier. A military train was due that evening, headed for Wau. If the brigadier agreed, they'd tie the grain cars on. Now please follow to where they would dine.

"He's chased up a bloody army shipment? Rifles and ammo for our very own General Adide! What more shall we ask for? Dining car complete with black waiters?"

Fix-It, he thought, worked for someone high up. They entered a dwelling, the floor spread with carpets. Women brought in stewed sheep's stomach with tomatoes, onions, chili. The bread *kisra*. Marsden chatting away, and Garang downed the obligatory *aragi*. Not a bad whiskey, this. Marsden negotiates, he thought, and I bond with the locals through drink.

"To the shirt," Garang said, toasting Marsden.

Marsden probed Fix-It. Would their grain be a problem for the army? Fix-It delivered the full teeth smile. It was the army's job to look after the refugee camp. Was there danger of attack by SPLA? *Murahaleen*? Fix-It's men would come along, provide an escort. And their Land Cruiser? Fix-It would load it into a rail car. Now the curtain across the door, flung aside. Enter the messenger, bearing the letter with the brigadier's seal. *Aragis* all round! Marsden declined. Therefore the Dinka doctor must drink instead!

"Marsden my man, are we not set?!"

"Let's hope we're not being set up," Marsden said. They headed for the Land Cruiser. "So the brigadier does us a favor—why?"

"Royalty comes through town, and you get up a parade. Kiss the arses of pale, washed out chaps like yourself, so that favors may be forthcoming. It pays all 'round to grease wheels. Did plenty of greasing myself, a nig in London."

The sun went down. The train rolled in. Marsden insisted they open one car. Fix-It barked a command. Two men appeared with lanterns, a saw. When the lock was cut, Fix-It slid the door open. The neatly stacked bags of grain resembled bees in their hive.

By the time the train began to move, the moon had risen. Marsden doffed the Christ of the Fishes shirt for a tee and lay down. Garang imagined triumphant return: barreling beneath flame trees, grain in tow, their colleagues surrounding them, cheering. The two lifted and carried above the heads of the crew. And there she would be, Garang thought, with that very kissable mouth of hers. Tamarisk, here I come!

You could close the book, and I could close the paper. But I need to know: Does this mom of the third dead son have a name? Fallujah, Mosul, Tikrit are tattooed on our DNA, but can I get the name of just one person? I want cell phone numbers. Vitals. Are there any sons left? Have they fled in order not to be dead? Why does death so often fall on progeny? The necessary sudden death could be visited on the elderly instead. We have a surplus of old farts, and so do Iraqis, though fewer. The free market should equalize supply and demand. The rep of the free market is at stake here, people! All because our whiskey of choice is oil.

The morning after Garang and Marsden's departure, a lorry of grain rolled in—serendipitous—so we had eats now for the skeletons. Marsden had deputized Beryl to woman the radio. Parrots brunched on gnats. Another scorcher was flexing its bicep. I prepared two coffees and headed to the office.

"Our UN man in Khartoum," Beryl said, "has christened me Lion." She mimed their radio exchange. "Giraffe to Lion?! *C'est vous?* So here's the scoop, pal. Our heroes hooked the grain cars to a train that was hauling Khartoum's ammo south to Wau. They loaded our Land Cruiser too. Then, middle of the night, some SPLA stopped the train."

Was this not precisely what I had feared!?

"The SPLA boys took Khartoum's ammo and the grain—and Garang. Drove him off in our very own Land Cruiser."

My love, flanked by guys with Kalashnikovs? Popped me in the boot, and off we went!

"Dinka doc for their bush hospital," Beryl said. "What a coup for the SPLA. Now they extort cash from his parents and Dinka expats. Plus he works his ass off in their surgery. He's a find, Annie—which means he's safe."

"Can you hear yourself? As though getting kidnapped is a feather in his cap!"

"He'll get the royal treatment. Want to bet he eats with the SPLA honchos?"

"Unless Khartoum attacks their hospital. Unless he walks on a mine. A refugee camp was robbed, Beryl. Get your head out of the sand!"

I wept. Beryl produced a hankie. There'd been a neatly packaged equilibrium: camp a tad claustrophobic, but there was the river. The choice of consorts limited, but I'd had the primo nifty lover. Now my herds slaughtered, my *tukul* torched. Parrots in the acacias squawked: Outrageous! Don't take it lying down!

"I have to talk to this Giraffe!"

"No need to roll out your nukes," Beryl said. She set me up with the radio, then went outside and hung with the parrots. I conjured Giraffe in his second-floor Khartoum office looking down at the street, Gaulois in one hand, Beaujolais in the other.

"*Dit-moi, chérie*," he said.

With breathy urgency I played up the amazing Giraffe's pivotal role. Freeing Garang from the dread SPLA depended upon him alone! In the formidable terrain of Sudanese politics, I implied, his capacity for manufacturing miraculous denouements was legendary. Giraffe was reassuring, *d'accord*. He would of course do what he could to persuade the SPLA to let Garang go. But since he'd spoken to Beryl there was more news. When I signed off and stepped out, I had a scoop.

"You don't look pleased, pal," Beryl said.

"In the few minutes since you spoke with Giraffe," I said, "more news has come in. The train and Marsden go on to Wau. And General Adide meets the train. Khartoum's already got news that the SPLA heisted their munitions. So they order Adide to arrest Marsden. On grounds that he conspired with the SPLA to pilfer army ordnance."

"Not a reprimand?" Beryl said. "Not an ultimatum? An actual arrest—of the head of an aid agency by the government he'd come to serve?"

I flashed on their departure. Marsden in the fishy shirt, a flag run up its pole. *Jallabahs* see that shirt, Garang quipped, and they fall on their knees.

"Annie, tighten your belt," Beryl said. "Your man and Marsden could both be gone awhile. Remember we're on African time here."

"You may be," I said. "I'm not."

Monyluak paced the edge of the volleyball court, his hands clasped, and wept. I went to work then, a Sappho fragment thrumming: "Him not here not here she hears him she sees him." At fourteen, Garang told me, he'd tried on toughness. Paced streets filthy with exhaust among pals—four blacks, two whites, a Bengali. They smoked, stole beer. "I watched *Zulu* five times," he'd said, "and walked my anger like a bloody dog." I flashed on his Levi's. He'd tossed them on top of my duffle. Some men's legs are not a turn-on—but his were. Suddenly, I was adrenaline. I dashed to the tent, lay on my back, and pulled the Levi's over me. Inert cloth infused by the imprint of his body! Oh rough mesh of cotton shimmering with meaning!

I had my grail. And it was ALL I had. It would have to get me through.

It's that moment portrayed on Etruscan vases: the lover in pursuit, reaching out, not quite able to touch the beloved's shoulder. You want them to go on in bliss? How do you think those depictions got onto those vases? The vases tell you: nothing lasts—which is why it's time to give up our daily oil martini!

What Annie's got is a pair of ordinary Levi's that she believes carries the imprint of Christ's body. But hey, whatever works. Everybody's got to make it through the night, including the mom of the third dead son. If I had the mom's cell number, I'd call and say there's cash waiting for you two at Bank One on the banks of the Tigris. Though is there a Bank One on the Tigris? I don't think so. Why are my charitable options so limited? I'm stuck with giving coffee money to this drunk lurching toward my table. He passes up the broker reading the *Wall Street Journal* and heads for me. I thrust out bills. In alcohol-enhanced gratitude he recites a rhymed quatrain, the gist of which is that God rewards people like me in the Afterlife.

Enough already, I say. Go get a cappuccino.

———

Garang woke in his hut in the hour before sunrise, fogged. Every morning they sent a kid to wake him. SPLA buggers who ran the bush hospital were short on everything, including sleep. Like bags of blood there was never enough. Sometimes he fell asleep wherever he was—in a chair outside his surgery, on the ground beneath that fig tree with its love birds. Once, midday, he'd lain down on a bed in the ward. Aluel, his nurse, did not rouse him. He'd waked when a wounded kid cried out.

How many blasted-open boys had he stitched? An assembly line, himself and two Dinka docs schooled in Nairobi. Three days might pass before the wankers got the wounded to him, and by then you could slice the stink with a knife. Petite Aluel cut away the bloody trousers. When the ventilator broke down, she chased up tubing, slid a length down the trachea. Her small hands squeezing the inflate bag, pumping the boy's breath.

The wound would have closed around bits of shattered bone, debris from the shell. He sliced open pink and yellow pustules: bile spurting like bilge. His clothes sweat-soaked. Aluel suctioning the mess so he could see.

These boys had risked death, and what had he risked? A quick cut to get at his appendix. In the West the pressing concern was the level of your cholesterol. Here, if you had a cholesterol level, you were among those with food.

At first, in the surgery Aluel had deferred: he was the *Turuk* surgeon, she underling. She'd maintained an edge: deferential and opaque. He'd danced his charm solo: ironic quips, extravagant exaggerations. She'd relaxed inside the poof of his clowning. Now she walked barefoot there, offering small sprigs of fragrant ease.

Khartoum's soldiers had attacked her Nuer village and rounded up the young women. Her mother ran toward them, screaming, fists in the air. A soldier hit her on the head with the butt of his rifle. I heard the sound as it hit, she'd said. My mother collapsed all at once. I could see, as she fell, her skull, cracked.

The soldiers kept the women—well bloody of course! But Aluel escaped, thanks to the handsome, dashing SPLA honcho Reik Machar. They'd fallen in love. This army, she'd said, is my family now. I am making a life here.

Reik Machar was John Garang's competition for leadership of the SPLA. John Garang insisted on a united democratic Sudan: bloody northerners and southern blues one grinning family. Reik, though, thought north and south should kiss each other good-bye. And the charisma of a bold Nuer leader may make a Dinka leader nervous. Garang had once locked Reik up—on grounds the man was plotting to off him—then relented.

"So marry your Nuer Reik then," he'd told Aluel. "Make him keep the peace between himself and John Garang. Cement the boys' alliance. Only way to win this war."

Her face, like a door slammed. "Fighting," she'd said, "is what they know."

Bloody true, of course. And he was stitching up blokes who knew little else. At Cambridge, on scholarship, he'd entered the mystery of healing. Entered—as the mystery unfolded, revealing itself—with reverence. Some things were established: the efficacy of antibiotics, the imperative of inoculation, the beneficence of transfusion. But beyond these certainties the terrain fuzzed out, turned conjectural, a swirl of accident, ancient practices, the immediacy of intuition. Medicine was mystery. You knew that to avoid septicity you had to provide immaculate sanitation. Simple enough, and yet the urgent requirement of performing the ritual resembled the imperative to bow before a god. Powers must be honored, appeased, and you hoped you knew the motions, the incantations, and their proper amount—lives would depend on it.

You knelt at the edge of the great swirling of two energies, darkness and light. Around the few stones of certainty the air curled, smoky, and you understood you did not know. You gave yourself into the hands of the invisible so that in surrender you might be guided toward whatever motions give rise to healing. Though he rarely spoke of this because patients wanted hope made of the flint of fact. Without that they came smack up against terror.

Beauty was in the faces. Flush of a boy soldier's face, of Aluel bearing a tray through the arch of the surgery door. But an army was not a landscape where he felt at ease. He called up the nineteenth century's Franz Binder, the richest European in Sudan. He'd manned river posts with his agents, devised the bargaining raid: attack a cattle camp, take animals, women, children, announce to whoever's left that you'll trade the captives back for ivory. And if they could not produce ivory, Binder took the women and cattle north. Now the sale of ivory had been banned—but this meant that elephants increased and trampled farmers' fields—which led to farmers killing elephants—which led to a shortage of ivory and made its value rise again. Now any bloke with a rifle could cash in. He sutured fighters so they might again go out and kill other soldiers, villagers—and elephants. For all he knew this Reik Aluel loved hunted those magnificent animals.

Was she Reik's convenience on those occasions when he came into camp? Suppose the bloke was hooked on power, that heroin? Men should not mistreat women, and this man Reik should put up or shut up: an expression the Americans used. A blunt phrase for a blunt people, though not the sort of thing his Tamarisk would say. He imagined her pouring a bucket of water over her blonde head. Would she put her hand between her legs and think of him? Of course! "I'll watch your ox go by," she'd said. "You'll make me your first wife."

He sat up: if he didn't move, they'd come get him. Thought you'd pop down to Africa and sprinkle a bit of progress 'round? Now you bloody well will, he thought. He reached for his towel and stepped out. It was still dark. Love birds dozed in the fig tree, and the figs were ripe: he could smell them. "I'll exchange this breast for the inside of your thigh," she'd teased. "Give me your mouth," he'd said. "Don't leave me bereft." He imagined writing to her. "Chow's adequate, Tamarisk, but lacks your mouth!" Though how write? There was no camel express. The honchos had let him radio the Khartoum office—Giraffe would inform his folks, and Marsden, lucky stiff, back in camp, would tell his Tamarisk. He flashed on her coffee cup, that grail from which she drank. He had mythologized this cup, its lip, that place where her tongue touched the glaze. He imagined her mouth, drinking. And when they rose from the dining hall table to go to work, he'd looked into the cup's bottom, cherishing the dark swirl.

Oh stop it! he thought. Making a fetish out of dank coffee grounds!

He recalled Fix-It's hand: that first gesture by which he'd claimed them. For better or worse he was Fix-It's done deal—which didn't include his Tamarisk! "Do you doctors fantasize about your patients?" she'd teased. Nothing had been said about fantasies of nurses. He'd fantasized beneath Aluel's dress—a castoff from the States—her body. He wrote it off: men do this, and so do women; it means nothing. Listen a mo, he told himself. Keep the demon sex out of it. His fingers, feeling for the chain around his throat, Annie's ring. She'd found the mum's bed empty. Her small hands smoothing the sheets—then the ring on the night stand, sealing her certainty: she'd been abandoned.

While you wear this ring, he thought, you cannot make love to another woman.

Image of lifting the chain over his head, laying it aside.

But he would not perform that dubious act. And besides— the mind a dog, utterly practical, surveying the possibilities— you've got no condoms, man! And if by chance you had one, chum, what would you bloody do? "I'm attracted to fools," Annie had said. A joke. Let me not, he thought, become a fool.

———

Now at the bottom of the page *another* Iraqi woman. One you expect, but two? This one looks like the great grandmom of the mom of the third dead son. She's an Akka in a voluminous black garment that I hope didn't come from Wal-Mart. Think crag and wrinkle bonanza and a Don't Mess With Me mouth. This face has been witnessing the works of humankind for the last thousand years. A jarhead has given her a box of U.S. military rations. The label states in English that the contents meet Koranic food laws. Does she read English? She balances the box on her head and looks past the camera at the surround. Coalition forces are moving into the neighborhood. She speaks to the mom of the third dead son. Get up from your flinging, daughter, because it's time to flee.

At dawn I heard the thud of mortars. Camp had felt impregnable. Now, no mistake, those were definitely mortars. Then that higher pitched sound: Kalashnikovs. The war, which had been reassuringly far off, had come close.

I stepped from the tent. A hurl of wind blasted through. This was unusual. We were lucky to get a breath of air when a parrot shot past. I headed for the showers. Bol with his towel over an arm raised one club hand in greeting.

"A red wind has come," he said. "In a red wind things are snatched up and hurled away. The red wind picks up our good soil and blows it north. Then it picks up the north's sand and blows it south. It blows our men north, and it blows *jallabah* soldiers south. Even mines come loose from the places where they were planted."

He turned his hands palm up—but there was no palm. His hands were knots. He looked at these knots. Then he turned them back down.

It was Day Eighteen Without Garang—and he had not sent a note clipped to the leg of a homing parrot. He would have if he could have, I thought, but Giraffe had warned. SPLA must not be in radio contact with UN camp—that would confirm conspiracy. The refugee women and their kids had flocked to him, he who was of them—and Brit. The word called up Whitehall, Charles and Diana. Not his father the barrister, his uncle the Tropical Med prof, University of London. I surged into resolve: my love was absent, but I would love his people. I waded through noon's billowing sheaves of heat to the warehouse and stood amidst heaped piles of bags. I singled out an especially plump pile and lay belly down across the pour and spill of food.

I loved the feel of food's bulk, its body. I'd told Garang how my mother refused the food I'd carried up the stairs to her. She would not accept my love or my need for love, and I'd turned my ardor toward my sister. See me at four ensconced in the armchair, tiny Felicia in the crook of my arm and in my other hand the bottle. She eats hungrily, and I'm amazed by this other mouth eating, myself looking down at this small girl in wonder, filling her.

I pleaded to be allowed to give her the first bottle of the morning, and the next and the next. I was the one who held the bottle at the angle that kept the milk coming, the one who talked the solicitous, encouraging talk, tonal and insinuating, of the mother with her infant. The act of feeding shimmered. It was as though I fed her from my body.

It was like being God, knowing you are nothing without your creation.

Now I see it so clearly: I was going to become a feeder. I was in Sudan because I wanted to love the world, and now it was time to feed my line. I stood up, walked out of the warehouse, and crossed the compound to my table, where the people Garang called "the skeletons" had lined up. Look, I thought, at these hungry people. They will not refuse your food: feed those ravenous mouths.

———

This can't go on. I can't go on writing this. If there were a Bank One, would anyone in their right mind leave their house and go into the street? You'd be saying, Here I am; I long to die. Angelic hosts are looking out for these women if they make it to the outskirts. And what would they do with cash in the desert? Bribe idle insurgents to drive them to the border? Insurgents don't have time to arrange transport. Do insurgents even possess transport? Their honchos do, but these honchos are not going to hand the keys to their one BMW copped from the Canadian Embassy to women. And does the mom of the third dead son have a driver's license? Because coalition forces will want to see it. And how will they cook kosher rations in the desert? Do they have a Primus Himalayan Multifuel? A Jet Boil Personal Cooking System, which boils water in two minutes? I don't think so. Is there even water in the desert? You can see the lists of extinct species out ahead, the scientists shouting that the enemy oil is at the gates—

The stars shimmered. The soldiers' fires blazed. Garang listened: men singing about a gun. Kind of song they'd sung to cows before cows went missing, Great Bull Shake the Tassels on Your Horns now turned into Great Gun Blast the Enemy's Bones. But the gods of this sorry place had chased him up—piece of luck!—a gift. Naguib the olive-skinned, his white *jallabiya* swaying like the robe of a god. Days Naguib wore camouflage, but nights he assumed his true identity. No one else here was Arab and light-skinned enough to be called green.

He was the SPLA's wild card, the Islamic scholar who'd defected from Khartoum, become the rebels' spokesman. He swept into the conference rooms of international councils, elegant in his command of English, quoting Shakespeare or Conan Doyle, Hammerskjöld or King, Marx or Madonna. He was as odd in this place as Michael Garang—though Naguib had chosen this.

"I have brought something to smoke," he said. "We will lace pleasure into the bloodstream and fuel our conversation."

"Without you and these smokes of yours I'd be knackered!"

"The leaders prefer alcohol. And they are addicted to white bread." They sat beneath love birds roosting in the fig tree. "White bread stands for all things from the West which northerners covet. Brits taught this to upper-class Arabs, and it filtered down. So to keep the populace serene, government fixed the price of bread low with a subsidy. Now the Sudanese pound's inflated, and this subsidy costs one hundred million U.S. dollars annually. When the president raised the price of bread, there were riots." He paused. "This cigarette has made me very talkative. There, I am done."

They looked at each other, pleased by what they saw. Then tore into debate. North and south must learn to love each other, but the two would never work as one nation because the National Islamic Front would not simply dissolve, and the oil was in the south and NIFers were addicted.

"This country is like a bad marriage," Naguib said. "North is husband, south the wife. North wants to rule the roost. Keep the woman down on the farm."

"And the oil's her dowry. If she leaves him, he's got to give the bloody dowry back to her father."

"Precisely. He doesn't want the wife to learn computer science, kiss him good-bye. This is a man who keeps slaves. He's unaccustomed to changing nappies." He passed the joint to Garang. "The north's soldiers—and ours!—look like roosters strutting."

Weed swept them into laughter's spasm.

"The world is ruled by roosters," Garang said. "We chickens are their subjects."

"Subject chickens!" Naguib roared. "Hail to roosters! God save the roosters!"

"Thatcher is a rooster," Garang said, "but now she's roosted."

"Think of it—a Gadhafi rooster! A Saddam rooster!"

"And rooster billionaires!" Garang said. "A Donald Trump rooster!"

When their laughter abated, Garang lay on his back. Naguib of the silver words, he thought, the wide mind, the broad heart. "Tell me, friend, how you came here."

"My people took black women and did not think what would happen. How these women were like a drop of darkness falling into water. How water took this darkness in, as a woman will caress herself with scented oils and the pleasure of the scent suffuse her. So that there came to be this place where darkness colored the water with its rich dye. I find that mixing of colors beautiful. This becoming each other with our blood. Identity is fluid, and such ceaseless moving appeals to me. But to others what flows feels frightening. Some Arabs have generations of slaves in their families, and now they wish to deny they are offspring of slaves. So they become hard-line. That is the form their denial takes.

"I was a lecturer at Khartoum University. My family is respected, and there is a large opposition to the government, so my father and I speak truth. Then government sent thugs to sack my office. I knew many Dinka men at school. We had become like brothers talking how to live together. So there came that day when I walked by the river and thought of my father's voice reading the Koran. How leave him and my mother? She taught me always to tell the truth, and if I got less than top marks, she scolded, Think what you are doing to yourself! As a child I was spoiled, and I ran to her friend Zeinab next door and begged her to tell my mother to be gentle with me. When my mother came looking, Zeinab said, Don't hurt this boy! He is your treasure! And my mother hid her laughter, took me by the hand, and said,

Come, my treasure, it's time to go home now." He laughed. "How I played the heartstrings of those two women!

"Then I walked beside the river and decided to go to my Dinka brothers. My father saluted me. He hates the government. My mother tried to joke: I taught you to be scrupulous—now look what you do! They know they won't see me again unless we meet in another country. I went with their blessing and did not stop loving them or they me. If you, my friend, decided to serve the SPLA and leave your family, you would not stop loving them." He lay his hand over Garang's. "So we cannot be sad. We are always inside that great love."

Surely once or twice Garang has done something disgraceful? But no, he's a Garang. Garangs are the bright spots, and good guys don't make for satisfying conflict. What's needed is AA for conflict junkies. Learn to live without conflict, and hummingbirds will thank you. Do hummingbirds have conflict? They disdain conflict! Blue whales also will thank you, as will sequoias. As some poet said, "Let the trees be consulted before you take any action." Think of it—you could get the Nobel Peace Prize for your Stop Reading campaign! You're Wo/Man of the Year, photo cover of *Newsweek*, right up there with JonBenet Ramsey.

Day 29: The heat, as usual, was ardent. Monyluak, as usual, paced the volleyball court's edge, weeping. The flat plain of southern Sudan, as usual, was flat all the way to the horizon. I imagined a teeny movement appearing on the horizon, motion that might be a migrating hartebeest but that would gradually become more visible and turn into a tall, gorgeous man with the longest legs in Sudan—

Quickly the UN Gatorade disappeared. We substituted a mix of sugar, salt, and soda and kept calling it Gatorade. There'd been plenty of F100 Big Milk for babies, but now it was gone, so we went with the standard milk.

Hunger, Africans said, is a hyena you've swallowed. It eats you from the inside out. It hurts slowly. Lash by slow lash it flays you. Your flesh goes and leaves bone shame. You feel that you are unworthy, and though you can't think what you did wrong, you are wrongness personified. Your being alive is a blight on civilization.

Again we ran out of *raau*. Beryl radioed Giraffe. I imagined him Gaulois in hand. Lorries, *chérie*, had left Khartoum a week ago.

There'd been a flurry of inoculating. Please no measles, and pray no cholera—that required quarantine. And double please no *kala-azar*, that madness. When a Dinka got it, they tied the guy to a tree to keep him from murdering. If Garang were here, I thought, he'd lighten things with a riff. "You think we foreign devils do death's work exporting nasty weapons? Wait until you see the new line of imports—plague for Paris, locusts for Bonn. TB developed in Azerbaijani prisons, on its way to Stockholm, Tokyo, Toronto. You won't have to go abroad to get your malaria; just stroll down to the deli! St. James's Special, courtesy of the Queen."

"The white wind is coming like a mafia boss," Nyanbol said. She wore solemnity like her white blouse, that perky yellow kerchief. "This wind stands over a person and looks down. What's here? Anything for me? It coaxes, as though to offer a sweet, until the sick one rises up to say yes. Then the white wind gobbles that person. Afterward its mouth is greasy. The white wind does not care what country you come from. If you go in its stomach, you will not come out."

At noon the parrots burst from the acacias and flew mad dash out of the compound—and the white wind sauntered in. It began to eat one baby at a time—

This can't go on—

"Tonight the white wind will eat all night," Nyanbol said. "Because it is white, it relishes darkness. What better time to stuff its white stomach. Even its feces are white."

Mid-morning more skeletons began to pour in. Beryl directed us to rig all the tarps for shade. Quickly the shade was full. I waded through Africans' pain, filling cups with Gatorade, and did not think about the fact that camp was filling up. A young man who'd hiked four days to get to us hauled in the latest story. Some northern soldiers had locked sixty-two Nuer in an ammunition storeroom. One soldier backed a tank up to the storeroom and turned off the motor. Others attached the tailpipe to the storeroom's vent. Then they stood around smoking. What did they say to each other? Maybe a soldier said, This is crazy. Maybe another one said, Hey, this isn't an order. Though maybe it had been an order. In armies men did that to each other. Imagine the soldiers standing beside the tank, smoking, debating. Though there came a point when the debate was over. One of them—which one?—put out his cigarette, climbed into the tank, and turned the motor on.

I walked around holding the story like an infant I was trying to settle. The stories came inside me as though I'd swallowed food. They were becoming part of my sinew and fiber, binding me into this place the way the food grown in a certain location binds you to that terrain. Inside the thud of mortars, that bass, I poured Gatorade. The bony woman before me wore a sling. Each rib stood out. Her breasts wizened nubs. The mother's eyes had gone into submission. My mother near the end, I thought, must have looked like this. You are looking at the woman your father, trying to protect you and your sister, didn't want you to see.

To keep myself company I replayed a Garang scene. Once back before the break-in I'd looked in at his surgery. Hell was flies buzzing, a little girl sitting on the examining table, stick legs dangling. A guinea worm wiggling out of the flesh of her calf. Garang knelt, winding the worm around a tongue depressor. You wait out months of pain, then the worm decides to come out, and you have to let it, so more pain. You couldn't pull on it for fear of tearing it in two.

"Give me a mo, Tamarisk. Think we're near the end here."

He chatted the girl up in Dinka. She bit her lip and nodded. All those months she'd had no morphine. She'd earned a PhD in pain.

When the worm ended, he patched her up, doused her with antibiotics, and sent her off.

"Sometimes I can't stand it," I said. "Sorry we can't put back that rainforest, guys, but here, have some Cheerios and a Pepsi!"

He'd touched my forehead with his. "On the head, love."

"Long live SAR11," I said. "Solidarity forever."

He'd slapped my hip. "I'll feel you up under the table at chow."

A memory is not a chocolate truffle, but it will have to do because the cooks have run out of truffles. All we have time for now is a quick description of the coup in Khartoum. Giraffe radioed the nookie: the National Islamic Front had infiltrated the army, arrested General Fathi, stolen his code, and used it to order army units to seize key points and the radio station. By the time officers learned that the army had been duped, the coup was a done deal.

Khartoum was chaos—and fear. Giraffe praised the Muslim manufacturer who bargained to get the Dinka corporal released from the ghost house. And the professor of Arabic who condemned the fatwa against the south. And the civil servant who harbored Anglican priests in his home when the crowd of fundamentalist youths massed at the cathedral, hurling stones. But the bulk of the citizenry had gone inside, closed the shutters. Few dared inquire about a disappeared neighbor.

So one more fundamentalist, militant regime takes over the fundamentalist, militant regime before it, and the war is still a war for oil and for food. Hence the popular ditty: You're trash without a Kalashnikov. Get some cash with a Kalashnikov.

Possibly you know what's going to happen now. The land is breaking down, the locust storms will resume, and that means bye-bye to your modest *raau* crop—if there was enough rain to grow a crop, which you'd have planted if you weren't terrified to go into the field and plant because at any moment soldiers might swarm through.

And things are going to get a lot worse for the southern Sudanese Peoples' Liberation Army. That the SPLA exists at all at the end of the eighties is thanks to Ethiopia's warlord president Mengistu. Outside Addis Ababa his stockpile of armaments had nailed down the huge plain. Rank upon rank of helicopter gunships, squadrons of bombers, warehouses filled with rifles, mortar shells, mines. Mengistu had set up camps for Dinka and Nuer fleeing southern battlefields and gave them tools, seeds, cattle. And he let the SPLA's John Garang set up training camps in the safe haven of Ethiopia. All very cozy, but Mengistu won't last. There will come a time when he has to run across tarmac to board his private plane and flee—

"Reik has abandoned me," Aluel said.

She looked—not to put too fine a point on it—bloody awful. No breeze. The muggy prevailed. He'd become her confidant. Who else in this hellhole? John Garang and Reik had patched up their fight—then the coup in Khartoum. The new president was a General Bashir, and General Bashir declared Sudan an "Islamic state." The war was now an official jihad, and dissenters could expect flogging, amputation, stoning, hanging.

And had this new government lured Reik with a bribe? You could bloody well bet on that! He imagined—nay he knew. He'd read history: Brits were the adepts at turning violence against them onto those they wished to divide and conquer. And so were those Khartoum honchos. When Dinka John Garang first organized the SPLA, some Nuer who'd fought Khartoum in the first war refused to join. John Garang got pissed and took down a Nuer leader, Samuel Gai Tut. It was said that after Gai Tut's death his body was given eighty lashes each day until there was nothing left.

Now it would be Nuer against Dinka. We will tie the Dinka, Reik and his honchos will say, and cut them with our knives. We will pierce them with our spears. We will tie them and burn them. We will rape the women and beat them and burn them. We will strangle them and hang them from trees. We will disembowel them and their women and their children. We will make them drink their own blood.

"Reik is John Garang's enemy now," Aluel said, "and I am Nuer, like Reik."

"Leave this army," he said. "You're way better than this place."

And where in bloody hell was it that he thought she could go?

Aluel stood. "I am going now. I am very tired."

Ditto yours truly, he'd thought. Aluel and I, we're the bloody slaves here. He watched her walk away: her smallness looked fragile. He stayed in the eave's shade and drank a glass of water. He'd put to bed the day's allotment of blood-soaked boys. Poor sods, hauling through blistering heat to the next ambush. The mind, honed by fear, narrowed and became a weapon. At night they drank, looked over the women, and took one.

Dusk drifted in, and John Garang arrived wearing camouflage and the red beret. He reviewed his troops, brought forth the rousing speech. Then he closeted himself with his commanders and Naguib—minus Reik. After mess the *miseria* flowed. Drums meant for dancing became political tools, beating up the notion that to die was glorious. Way to press gang impressionable boys into savagery. And the north's generals would trot out the very same rally and strut. North and south besotted, both having it off with an illusion. And now, because Reik and John Garang had quarreled, Nuer and Dinka would go at each other's throats.

Though the true backhanders were not this sorry army tied together with string and wire, nor those jihad *jallabahs* with their tattered Antonovs patched up with a few quid from abroad. The real backhanders were the brass hats, the Mr. Bigs. The ones you couldn't touch—and who wouldn't touch you. He thought of those black men in Handsworth, burning shops owned by Asians: this, his father warned, is what whites could drive you to, if you failed to understand.

Love birds in the trees riffled their green sequins. He stepped beneath the dusky ambience of figs. The air odorous, as though a woman, perfumed, stood beside him and plucked the fruit. To his narrow pallet, then. To the mind's hand letting go its grip: to blessed sleep. Their bloody war would bash on without him watching.

It was sometime after midnight when he heard Aluel's voice—urgent: Lummey! He pulled on pants, felt for the flashlight. Stepped out. She bent over, clutching her belly.

"You must sew me!" He lifted her and ran, kicked open the door, laid her on the table. Unlocked the cabinet—the ampules. "Have you back together in twenty minutes! Let the pretty drug take you off."

"I am their war zone!" she said. Sobbing.

He talked while he scrubbed, put on gloves, soothing her until she was out. Then cut away her sopping skirt. A surface wound across her belly, just deep enough to leave a scar. It would be easy to stitch the edges in place. In surgery the body became landscape: curve of a rise, tapering of a limb like the downslope of a hill. He gave himself to the task and did not think. Then he was done. He'd tied off the last suture. Then washed the wound again the way you'd lave detritus around a fossil so that you could see its pattern. Their war zone, she'd said. Now he saw. The men who'd held her down had not so much cut as etched on her belly the emblem of this place—emblem burned into the psyches of boys whose school was war. He stared at his handiwork, neatly emphasizing the image that would heal into a scar: the butt and barrel of your state-of-the-art automatic rifle.

Shock is titillation. It gets the adrenaline moving. It fuels urgency, and your mind tosses up the adage: this is not a dress rehearsal. I imagine you impatient for conflict to kick in. I imagine you getting up, wanting a snack, wanting to drink something, wanting to check out your photo in Facebook or cruise around MySpace. Desire is endless, it leads to endless restlessness, and now you read while you wait to board. In the air you read hard so as not to consider the fact that this could be the flight that takes you down. The body loves being alive; it wants to be eating, sleeping, fucking, working, whistling in the shower, getting dog tired, putting off looking for a job, putting off doing taxes, putting off going for the gold—and reading instead.

Someone asks you what's been happening, and you can't think: how *did* those days go by; what was I doing? I can't have been reading all that time. Then just when you don't expect anything, a sudden epiphany of joyous awareness of all those rills of pleasurably being alive floods you, and you swear never to go unconscious again.

Which doesn't last. You go back to reading.

You're reading when you could be swimming in a lazy circle with parrot fish, or chatting with a blue jay, or lying in grass sending up sky praise. You could be divesting. You could live smaller, easier, lighter, sweeter.

The more you own the less you give, and the less you own the less you sweat.

Then it will be necessary to grow some food, and you will gather with others and get your hands dirty in the good, hard earth. Which, if you can clear your consciousness of the detritus of electronic hype, you will like.

Then you'll die.

Meanwhile those species of hummingbirds Brian Doyle lists in his essay—the bearded helmet-crests and booted racket-tails, violet-capped wood nymphs and violet-tailed sylphs—sixteen species in all, not counting the ones they hadn't yet identified—went extinct on your one—yes, one—typical day.

"We're full up," Beryl said. She ordered the gate closed. Outside the chain-link Africans massed. Their limbs were tinder. Just after noon the flame trees shaded a bit of earth outside the fence, and if you were able to get in there, you joined the elite, and who knew: the *Turuks* might open and take you in. Slowly this shade slid across the outsiders. More elbowed in. The shade bulged. But by mid afternoon this shade had moved back inside. Those outside stood again in full sun. We carried Gatorade out, and these skeletons drank ravenously.

Bol walked the inside of the chain-link like an ambassador explaining why his country cannot accept more immigrants. His mangled hands hanging, a helplessness.

I watched a doc standing in the infirmary doorway facing the compound. Though his hands had excised the tiniest of polyps, they were huge and empty. One by one the mothers came. Into his hands each one laid a small corpse. Sometimes, he told me later, a mother's face looked like a crushed blossom. But sometimes her face was blank. She was hungry and weary, and three of her children had died, and now here was another.

He looked at each dead child as though it were necessary to see it thoroughly. He watched the backs of the mothers going away. The backs of those mothers looked raw, as though flayed.

The white wind finished the babies as though they were hors d'oeuvres. It swallowed kids who should have been in primary school. Then it took a man in its white hands and stuffed that man into its white mouth and ate that man with its white teeth. The white wind went on, woman after woman, man after man.

I wore a dress made of numbness. Evenings we lay the dead on bed sheets and carried them to the far edge of the tarmac. Hyenas assembled and moved a little back to give room. We rolled the dead onto the ground. I flashed on Garang's remarks the first time we'd walked to the river. Hyenas' jaws, he'd said, were vises for crushing bone. Their teeth grinders for grinding bone. And in their acid bellies bone dissolved.

We were stretched, but that was part of the job. Hyenas were part of the job. The stories were definitely part of the job. What I thought was that the stories would keep coming in, lorries would keep rolling in, and we'd keep feeding my lover's people. That was how the UN operated, ever onward. God himself could not halt the World Food Program. Even if we gringos were to run out of supplies and go hungry for a day or two, the war would move past us and further south, mortar fire would fade and lorries roll in—and Garang would come back.

And if things got to a point where camp had to close, we'd fly out drinking Black Label and munching brie.

I was of the privileged. I would be taken care of. Though the people around me did not have that privilege—they counted themselves lucky to be alive. The day before, I'd accosted Monyluak pacing and weeping, and put it to him.

"Mony, what are you weeping for? Are you in physical pain? Can we get you a med of some kind?"

He looked at me, gauging me, and then, slowly, he smiled. "My tears," he said, "they are good ones. My tears, they are for the knife of sweet life."

On the memory of that wave of Mony sweetness I took a luxurious shower. After dinner Beryl dangled the Land Cruiser keys. We'd had two vehicles, one of which the SPLA had swiped along with my man.

"Battery needs charging, pal. Let's go for a spin."

"What a daring idea," I said. "Do we head south to Wau? North to Khartoum?"

She grinned. We climbed in. We were fagged from work, its relentlessness, and we hadn't been chatting much. Now a child's wail squiggled across the air.

"Imagine," I said, "having a kid in a war."

Beryl put the key in the ignition but did not turn it. "We're at war in the West, but we frame it as issues. Drugs, domestic abuse. Police brutality. Then we package the stuff and export it." She turned to me. "I can't focus on a partner now, because I'm still looking for Serena."

"*Serena*!?"

"My disappeared daughter. She was five. I can't say more. I can't think about it."

I took Beryl's hand, and we sat at the edge of a blackness going down into the earth. I flashed on a pit beneath a rest stop toilet where a man dumped a girl with his trash.

"Oh Beryl," I blubbered. "You never said!"

"I keep it back burner. But now and then it sneaks up to the front burner."

"Like now," I said. "Those damn mortars, and the stories—"

I blubbered on, the name Serena flowing into the image of my mother's gaunt face. I was fresh out of the shining ability to pull myself together.

Beryl turned the key. Nothing. She tried again.

"I don't believe this."

She got out, lifted the hood, wiggled the battery connections, got back in. Tried again. Nothing.

We climbed down.

Across the compound I saw a woman holding a child's white Chevron tee looking up at the sky. Paradise might be up there, flourishing. But we were in southern Sudan, on the vast ground.

You imagine this is foreshadowing disaster. There's disaster in Kazakhstan, where 367 seals died this spring along the Caspian Sea coast due to canine distemper virus—which seals would be immune to, had their immune systems not been compromised by some noxious chemical invented to make bucks and give blokes a job.

And the doomsday clock has moved forward another minute.

And this Iraq thing entails oil fires, inland oil spills, and ten-year-olds with breast cancer from depleted uranium weapons. We have the trillions to do it, so we do it. And the ice, which you don't give a damn for because you want to drive so that you'll experience the high you get from speed—that ice doesn't give a damn for us either.

Meanwhile you're hooked on your nightly bowl of Netflix. You avoid your century's challenge: lifestyle transformation. The cattle, pigs, sheep, and chickens we munch produce more greenhouse gases than the transportation sector. Cultivate your gardens, and kill the developers! Time to get a composting toilet, people! Up with condoms! Adopt a Korean orphan! Get a sledgehammer and beat your coal-fired power plant, which puts out more carbon than all of Manhattan, back into plowshares. Yes, I'm a harridan. If you don't like it, close the book.

A scorcher of a day, and he'd become a bloody saltern! Now love birds searched out perches for the night. The full moon had risen. Aluel slept in the infirmary. He sat beside her guarding that sleep. Subject peoples, unable to extricate themselves from tyranny, in frustration turned on each other. It was human, and humans did not learn from history. Aluel's face the face of a girl who'd heard her mother's skull crack. People tried to mend, to spring back, and sometimes a version of innocence reappeared. You needed to believe the world was, if not benign, still a place the benign might visit.

And had the backhanders who carved also raped her? He'd stitched the wound and refrained from examining her.

To live not simply with a scar, but *this* scar, bloody ugly in its message: force reigns. You might hide it—until you undressed: then there it was, absolutely foul and fucking unfair, a mockery of your integrity. And if in glad abandon you took a lover, in those urgent moments of first undressing, how explain? Or bathing with your child, that moment when the child saw, asked.

Naguib had arranged to transport Aluel to Nairobi. Since the coup the SPLA was in retreat, the hospital done for. No antibiotics, dressings, disinfectant—and no ampules. They'd brought in a boy, leg blasted, too weak to survive amputation. Michael had begged a bit of the honcho's Napoleon. "Give the kid a drink for the road."

He thought of that fish he'd eaten at mess. Its shimmering slipperiness, its leap upward toward light. Now that light was inside him, becoming him, his body destroying the fish's body, making its substance over into his. Was that what men wanted? To make the world over in their image? Armies were got up by *Homo sapiens*, those offspring of the first hominids who'd stood upright, devised stone tools, researched front-to-front sex. *Rudolfensis, habilis, erectus, Australopithecus boseii* had hung out in east Africa for thousands of years like the alien species in that Star Wars bar, playing video games. Then *erectus* grew a bigger, more complex brain and wandered, munching veggies, fruits, and tenderloin and spreading their kind. But where *sapiens* wandered in, other species fell away. *Sapiens* ate them or killed them for sport or simply gobbled all the produce. We were still at it, he thought, in our unconscious, methodical way.

And the more spaciousness shrank, the more we invented reasons why some of us were nifty but others a sorry lot. So that finally—gauntlet thrown down—we were at each other's throats. And even while we tore at each other, we were busy making more of us and munching our way toward disaster. The fabled intelligence of *Homo sapiens* was a wash. What we are, he thought, is ignorant and crafty.

He left her and went out under stars. The image rose of his Tamarisk at work, the stories coming in, haunting, the daily dealing with that tax accountant the heat. How's the place ticking over without me? They were bound by the heat: it was the same heat here as where she was; he imagined the two of them sweating at the same time, a kind of bodily camaraderie—though at a remove. This remove, he told himself, was trifling—but had the devil's own job getting himself to believe it.

Soldiers had carried the patients away on stretchers, and the Dinka doctors walked away with them. And how far would those soldiers carry those stretchers? At some point they would lay the stretchers down and go on.

Thanks to Naguib John Garang had agreed to leave the doctor the Land Cruiser and a driver. He flashed on John Garang's pressed fatigues: you could bet the big bull didn't do the pressing. He saw Naguib's white *jallabiya* swaying toward him through the dark, tambour in one arm and in the other a bottle.

"Lummey! You've scotched us some Napoleon?"

"My heart is heavy," Naguib said. "We must soothe ourselves."

The Napoleon sweet as his Tamarisk's mouth. "Top drawer!"

Naguib held the tambour as though it were a woman he loved. The tambour's sound wound around them. At first the music shifted, running in, then retracting, thrusting hard, then dying away. But a melody kept reasserting itself like a trapped animal looking for a way out.

Then the opening, and it slid through.

The music turned, climbed upward: sadness laced with the joy of release. A sound to turn the faces of its hearers toward stars. Naguib, Garang thought, was meant to soar, glide in long, lazy loops, settle on some high precipice.

When the final note died away, the two drifted, buoyed. Their silence a way of kneeling before the music.

"Friend," Naguib said. "Life wounds us, so that our hearts may open. Only the wounded know how the heart may feel both this world's ugliness and its beauty."

Naguib, he thought, did not want to lose him—as he did not want to lose Naguib. "You'll pop up to London for a meeting at some point, and I'll pour the drink."

"Of course I will come, God willing. But now, my friend, I bring you news which will be painful. This heat in my country breeds fanatics. People go around in trance, open to visions. But these visions are their own illusions. They float off into fantasy and become enamored of asceticism and start denying themselves. They elevate denial into religious practice. They want to become saints, but they don't have the hearts of saints, only their own distorted notion that the saint is a holy man who doesn't touch women and drinks only water. The long afternoon siestas become the breeding ground of nightmares. An imam tells them they are the pure surrounded by the impure, and that these impure do not honor Allah. And they beat themselves and say yes, those others are evil; we must drive this evil out. In an instant one hundred thousand men rush off to do savagery.

"This government—before the coup—arrested your friend Mr. Hargreave. They believe he conspired with us to steal the army's ordnance."

"My Aunt Fanny! We had the permit—signed and sealed."

Naguib took a sip and swallowed slowly.

"Marsden's in Khartoum then?"

"Yes. He was."

Had something happened? It may have done—

"Now this new General Bashir has performed his execution."

"Burked him? Can't have done!"

Humiliation flooding him: he'd pushed zipping up to Baba, while Marsden watched—amused and charmed. Charm, that MO he'd perfected in order to ingratiate himself with whites. "This is so damned male of both of you," his Tamarisk said.

He sat very still and wept.

"You imagine your heart is broken," Naguib said. "But it is broken open."

It's not just women now flinging themselves down, sobbing. Now men also sob. You see it every other day in the papers, on the tube. Men in rage and sorrow, sobbing. I did not make up this execution. This is based on historic fact. Khartoum offed an aid worker suspected of cozying up to the SPLA. In the end we will all be alike. Death is closure.

And has it occurred to you that life is one closure after another? These three-thousand-year-old eyes of Akka's look past me into distance. It's clear where our values lie. We have bad air and the finest lattes anywhere. You can see the lay of the land ahead: the more the world powers make war, the richer the rich will get and the poorer the poor, and thus more and more employees of Feed the Children and Concern will fuck more and more—because it's not going to get better, not in Africa, and today could be the first day of the rest of your life—or the last.

And what are you doing on this last day?

You're reading, thinking that at any moment conflict will kick in.

Mortar boom, blat of rifles.

The lorries had not arrived.

The Land Cruiser had not kicked on.

We had gringo food, but we'd had no *raau* to feed the Africans for a week, only Gatorade. Which meant carrying out more corpses for the hyenas. Bol walked the inside of the chain-link talking to the people outside. They banged the fence and accused Bol of subterfuge. They knew we gringos were eating, and they suspected that there was *raau* in that warehouse, if only they could storm in and look.

Just to be inside the fence would make them feel safer.

A fence was protection, and the closer you could get to the pink gringos, the more likely you were to survive.

I poured Gatorade and looked into the faces, one by one, making the oh-so-important eye connection, seeing that person so that they would feel recognized, counted. The faces one after another a slow mantra, and each face was herself, himself, and also him: my Garang—

You can see the Darfur thing out ahead. At the end of a tunnel bored into the center of a mountain on an island near the North Pole, Norway is constructing a bunker for a doomsday seed archive of the world's 1.5 million crops. Meanwhile twenty-six thousand gallons of Exxon Valdez oil go on polluting Prince William Sound, the oil fires burn, and scientists teach rats to fear two different musical tones by torturing them with electrical shocks, then use a drug to wipe away the memory of one of the tones—and the United States announces the selection of the winning design for a new nuclear warhead—

I can't go on; neither can Akka nor the mom of the third dead son; neither can the refugees—but we also aren't dead yet, so here we are, going on—

Near Bol a woman outside the chain-link wearing a baby's sling gripped the mesh. Beside her a man squatted, and the mom grabbed the link and climbed onto his shoulders. Slowly he stood and raised her up. She teetered on his shoulders, clutching chain-link with one hand, and with the other she reached into the sling and lifted out a handful of baby. Her hold on this bit of flesh tentative, as though the baby was one of those precarious Dinka words about to disappear from the language.

Jostling and banging on the chain-link halted.

We'd closed the gate, no more skeletons could enter, but now there was this mother, the air around her hot and lit. The chalky sheath from the birth still on the baby. This small person had entered the world precipitously, possibly within the hour. Now the mom crouched, straightened, heaved. The baby arced over and down, and I caught it, barely, its chalky, slick covering slippery. I stood there holding this live event, a newborn infant, and around me a shout rose as though all those kept outside had stormed the gate and burst through.

You imagine Annie adopts the baby, one of her lover's people—hoping the baby will bring Garang back soon. But the child won't live: too tiny. And there's more bad news up ahead. Roughly two decades on from where our lovers pine, the head of the SPLA, John Garang, will negotiate a truce of sorts with Khartoum. The two, north and south, will agree to live five years as a confederation, and after five years southerners will vote on whether to join up with Khartoum as one nation forever or wave bye-bye. But soon after this plan is agreed upon, the SPLA's John Garang will board a plane, a plane that goes down in one of those mysterious crashes Africa is famous for—

The morning of leaving he and Naguib had risen with the sun and bathed. Naguib's paler body beside his blue-black, together inside the sound of water's splash.

"I could not rest," Naguib had said. "I am wounded by your leaving."

"You saved me from bloody boredom. Without you, I'd have turned ugly."

What he hadn't said: you taught me with your being, which is like music.

They'd walked into the thrust of heat. Naguib stood beside the Land Cruiser. Garang was conscious of the stillness, as though air suspended its motion.

"Now I must continue without you," Naguib said. "I am imagining now two strands of fiber from a baobab, pulled asunder."

What if he were not to meet Naguib again? Planes crash regularly in Africa; men step into the paths of Uzis. Why had he not, with his wordy mouth, declared his love?

"You said it for us when you played the tambour," Garang said. "We are never outside this great love that surrounds us."

Naguib took his friend's face in his hands then, as though to embrace the man whose face it was. He'd leaned in and kissed Garang's lips.

"Do not forget me, I beg you," he'd said.

Now it was two days on, bumping down this washboard Africans called a road, box seat square before that opera The Horizon. Himself in back, and in front the driver and an SPLA boy with rifle. He'd chatted up the boy—adolescent and shy at first. Then the kid got chuffed—ensconced in a vehicle, tooling the countryside! He'd started picking up Garang's lingo. "This road, bloody ball breaker!"

The memory of Naguib's face and of the field of his body rose. You could not know whose eyes would meet yours kindly, whose heart would take you in. When others turned from you, it felt as though their turning away cut you out. And if you accepted this distance as real, you brought it into being. It became, in your mind, a fact. But you could choose not to think this way. He remembered being a child in a sandbox, taking sand by handfuls, watching as it fell through his fingers. He lifted another handful, and in this lifting and letting go he'd felt purely happy. Sand a dear friend, a live thing that loved him, and he'd known that there was in him that tender, protected organ the heart, with which he also loved.

And love was not the Newtonian universe. It was the wholeness he remembered in the sandbox. Near dawn the morning of leaving, he'd risen into that series of moments in which it was no longer dark nor light. He stood in the hut's doorway. Before him now the sun was rising. Behind him the full moon set. As though the rising and falling of things met in a moment of wholeness. Between sky and sand he'd fit perfectly: he was the *axis mundi* stake at the earth's pole, the life around him thick, rich matter.

A Schrödinger's cat? Bugger that! The wary outsider London had trained him to be was gone. That Niagara tightrope walker had refused the mutually exclusive either/or, stopped in the middle of his walk over the falls, and cooked an egg—and in the quantum universe you ate the scrambled egg with relish and continued on. I'm not halved, he thought, but doubled. Fully Brit, fully Dinka, and more: a wave function, that hypothetical creature of infinite possible outcomes.

He imagined his Tamarisk asleep on her side, turned toward the space where he'd lain. But Marsden was dead. Would she understand his chagrin? Could she live with who he'd become?

Could he—Marsden's death burned into his DNA? Next to his black physician's bag lay Marsden's fishy shirt. When they'd boarded that train, Marsden changed to a tee. Now the shirt lay before him, its motif of palms, the leaping fish. How honor the dead; what would be fit ceremony? Slowly, with conscious deliberation, he put on the Christ shirt. Slowly he buttoned the buttons. Then he was weeping.

A line from Shakespeare rose: "O! pardon me, thou bleeding piece of earth, / That I am meek and gentle with these butchers."

The grain bags at that UN camp were stamped with an inscription: "This is a gift from the people of the United States of America." I want my mood to shift. I feel like being soft. Let's admit that we're generous when there's earthquake or flood. But do we recognize that the world can't be owned? To give back what we've stolen from Africa—the mind goes blank.

And do we have the *nous* to rise above fear?

Reader, a day may come when you decide to smash the mirrors, melt down the chassis and the missile hull. What is—this moment—goes on like those raucous parrots agreeing and disagreeing. Give yourself to that motion, and your small, single life grows large. This is the god ravishing us. You think gods can't? You think you're immune? Feel around: Is there a border? Tell me if you find any demarcation between yourself and those stars.

I'm telling you, Reader, the grain grows, stalks lengthening, each grain swelling, the sheath bursting the way the sun burns outward from its own flung heat. Imagine this grain longing to feed us, to hurl itself into the many mouths. Bring in hardship, and feed it; lie down with it, and kiss it. Put food in its mouth. The breath of the hungry blows toward us, enters us, becomes us. Wherever you are, this wind is blowing—

———

Giraffe radioed: Garang was coming! Beryl loaned me her binoculars.

"To bring your man closer sooner, pal."

In the last few days the sound of mortars had diminished. This argued that the war had moved a little away from camp, though how far away we weren't sure. I was glad not to hear that sound, and I went out beneath the flame trees onto the silence of the land, walking through noon heat's rippling mirage. I leaned into that heat as though it were my lover's body, and in the cathedral of my mind I set the bells swinging and bonging against each other, making a glorious noise. I was going toward him, each step bringing me closer, and I willed him to guess, surmise, know: Darling, I'm coming.

When, against the horizon's line, I made out his tall, lean body, I raised the binoculars: my Garang was wearing Marsden's fishy shirt. That shirt was SO not Marsden, but Garang had the chutzpah for it. I would tease him: you look like a tourist, darling, strolling the beach looking for a jiggle!

He saw me, thrust up his long arm, and waved. Then he began to run. The road to the camp curved, making the distance between us longer. To get to me sooner he plunged off the road and cut in a straight line toward me. I stood still, gazing through the binoculars, sating myself on the look of him: his body is a glorious thing, who would have thought it, there's nothing like it, milk for the eyes, heart's sumptuous meal—

He was still far enough away that if I were to lower the binoculars his features would blur. Far enough away that I saw the explosion before I heard the sound of the mine's detonation: earth spraying upward in arcs opening out like the petals of a flame tree's pulsing red blossom.

Then where he'd been, a slow cloudiness, billowing—

You say I shouldn't allow this?

Remember those Etruscan vases.

And just try clearing a minefield sometime.

I can't arrange events. I watch the world unfold and tell you what happens next. The king dies in a mine blast, and afterward the queen weeps and then files for a 501c3 and starts a charity in honor of the king: that isn't conflict.

The next time I hear the term "page turner" I just may scream.

Life is one moment after another, period.

Savor those moments.

My latte boots up Akka's three-thousand-year-old face as if it's carved on Rushmore. You can see where this is going. It's heading straight for cluster bombs, stretchers and intravenous drips, the nine-year-old boy with no legs, the moms sobbing. We're heading for body parts. Body bags. Graves.

Even the sandbox sweetie clings to his gun as if it's a blankie. My gun is mine. No, you can't hold it. Do you want to hold it? You can't. It's mine. Yes, you're my friend, but you can't hold it. Do you want to just look at it? OK, I'll take it out so you can look. Get ready. Here it comes. See? No, you can't touch it! Did I say you could touch it? I said no touching! Because you'll get it dirty. Yes, you WILL! You will not be really careful because you aren't careful. No, you can't touch it for just a minute! I told you why not. You're starting to make me mad!

You see where this is leading. It's leading to World War III. The kid with the gun loses it and whaps his little pal. Stop that right now! his mom says.

But he touched my gun!

I did not!

How did this start? the mom says.

It started when he hit me back!

Do girls make a fetish of their thingies? Yes, but girls also get naked and go dancing. Thus the old Celtic saying: never give a gun to a young man who has not yet learned to boogie.

IV

Beryl stands in line at the airport Starbucks to pay for our lattes, and I slip on her headphones. You might not think hard-headed Tell It Like It Is Beryl would go for Rumi, but Rumi is her other Black Label. "Eat on and on, you lovers, at eternity's table," Rumi says. "The feast is forever, and spread out for you." I listen, I who haven't lost a child. No besom sweeps away Beryl's longing for that daughter. That absence is like the dust in the photographs of nebulae—those shells of gas thrown off by dying stars. Telescopes picked up the signals still because once something was there.

"After Serena disappeared," Beryl said, "I decided: war is ubiquitous; it's in my face. So I'm going to turn it into its opposite. Each time I won a case I turned pain into good for another person. I was the girl in Rumpelstiltskin spinning straw into gold."

After the coup in Khartoum closed the UN camp, Beryl and I flew out to another aid job. Imagine flatness set with the grid of war: tanks in rows, armored trucks. Warehouses stocked with spare parts, ammo. Mines in crates. Thousands and thousands of machine guns. Howitzers. Ranks of hangars, and in the hangars ranks of bombers. Beneath this weight the land can't breathe. The soil lies prone beneath sun, dying slowly, and some of us go there and try to feed it and its people.

For the rest of my life this is what I will do.

We rise at dawn. While we bathe, cook, eat, light is a bank of voices fanning upward to sky. UN officials send e-mails, make phone calls, draft bills, but sometimes months pass before the suits ante up money and politicians give permission to fly food to the famine. But in the meantime there is always famine somewhere, and Beryl and I go there and do the work that isn't glamorous. We boil water, do laundry, feed the mouths that come, and look into their eyes, those beggars with their bowls.

Bad days are when one of us dies in a bus bombing or gets kidnapped. But even when things are bad, some of us appear with cauldrons of food, work assumes the shape of moving water, and the one who receives and the one who gives are a single being. And I have taken up Beryl's attitude. Now when I fill a bowl, I tell myself I'm turning the empty into the full.

Work polishes us to a high sheen like stones in the ocean, and at the end of a day tiredness is a silver gown no one sees, so thoroughly does it clothe the body. Sometimes I go to the warehouse where sacks of grain lay one against another and lie down among them. I call up the faces of those I've loved and feast on them, as I'll feast on the faces I haven't yet seen. For there are so many of us. All of us inside food's huge muscle, the world stomach—where we've always been, where we'll be until we die.

Old men watch their orchards burn; soldiers destroy the films in the children's TV station and run porn; and someone cuts an order, and the trunks of ancient trees lie on their sides. Women wail over the body of a child who killed himself, scavengers prowl looking for things to trade or sell, sometimes someone finds a body, and in cities at dusk people hurry past soldiers in riot gear. The walls inside the towers are screens people watch to try to forget how lonely they are, and Beryl and I go where the famine is and float amidst the hungry. Mama tired, the hungry say. Boy sick. Girl scared. We drink from the same bucket, the thirsty ones and I, and I don't have to smile, nor do they.

There were more stories. The story of one Dinka father who in his misery looked for a way to redeem Dinka people. If we want the help of gods, Nyanbol had said, we sacrifice a cow, and this man was drawn to the image of Christ's crucifixion. He got so fervent and mixed up by his pain that he killed his own son, thinking this would bring peace. His son: a cow, a Christ.

Some of the stories got added to. For instance, the story of the Baggara woman who'd married a Dinka. The woman hung from the tree surrounded by a crowd of curious Baggara, some of them her neighbors. Some of the men had been ordered to stay and guard the body until dark. At some point one of these men lay his rifle on the ground, stepped away from his cronies, and walked toward the tree. Was she still alive? Had he known her well, or distantly, or not at all? Her body turned slightly in the moving air. Her feet dangled. Slowly the man reached and took one of her feet in his hands. Slowly he kissed this foot. There was a tenderness in this slowness. How long did his lips rest on her skin? Then he let go and took the other foot in his hands and also kissed it.

And there was the story of a man in camp who entered the tent of a woman with a baby and begged her to feed him from her body. She said no: her milk was for that baby. But he asked again, and she looked at his face and felt how his hunger was like her own. So she told the man to lie beside her, and she gave him one breast. He drank fast and hungrily. Then he begged for the other. I cannot, she said. I am keeping some for my child. The man lay beside her inside that huge hunger that was their life, his and hers and her child's. He began to weep. And the woman lay beside this man and wept with him.

And Monyluak. Perhaps in the Kaukuma Refugee Camp he made a family, or found a way to use his sad gentleness to help others. Or perhaps he went to Nairobi, lived in the Kebira slum until his sores got worse, and went mad and died. I take out the memory of Monyluak's face and unwrap it. I look at it as Bernini would have if he were about to carve stone. And I wonder: Does Monyluak still unwrap the ear and look at it and remember that moment when he was spared and yet not spared?

In a variant version of Monyluak's story the soldiers grabbed hold of his friend and dragged him to where Monyluak stood. One of them gave Monyluak the machete and ordered him to cut off his friend's ear. A soldier placed the barrel of his gun against Monyluak's back at the level of his heart. Do it now, the soldier said. Monyluak did what he'd been ordered to do. Then he dropped the knife and fell to his knees weeping.

It was then that the soldier picked up the ear and placed it in Monyluak's hand.

V

I am an eater, admiring lettuces at the market, longing to taste what steams in the pot. I feel food going into my stomach where it begins to become my body, and I know that eating is the beautiful destruction. Yes, we are destroyers. We transform the thing we destroy and are transformed by it. Praise to destruction that creates us. Praise to creation that makes us destruction's meal.

Sometimes I carry on a conversation with my mother as though she were alive. Mother, I say, I wonder about your mother. I never knew this grandmother, who died before I was born. But in Rome I came across some research. If the mother of an anorexic feeds her daughter with her own hands, spoonful by spoonful as though she were a baby again, that daughter can recover.

I imagine Felicia and I in that bedroom with you and the grandmother we'd never seen. This grandmother holds a bowl of butternut squash soup, the aroma wafting across the air. She lifts a spoonful to your mouth. We watch your mouth open, close, swallow. We hold onto each other and keep watching, and our grandmother keeps feeding you, and you keep swallowing. I imagine we watch you eat until the bowl is empty.

Mother, pietà at the center of my life, my father took you away from the house because he didn't want your daughters to see how skeletal you were. And perhaps this was for the best, because I flourished. I became a hearty eater, relishing the feel of food going into my stomach, where it begins to become my body. I tell myself that this is the best way to love you, this is what you would have wanted for me.

Now I mourn you and honor you by consorting with the hungry and feeding them into fatness. And I feed myself as well and grow pleasantly plump. How I wish you could see me, hear me. Know me. If you were here, Mother, I would say, Look at me now; see how I flourish.

Look, Mother, and be astonished.

Look at me and see who I have become.

VI

The night before we left the UN camp, Larry McBride tooled in. He arrived at the office with Chevron Scotch and a bucket of ice and proceeded to the generous pour.

"To Michael Garang and Marsden Hargreave. Damn fine men."

He told us that he'd gone to the prison, and with a hefty bribe courtesy of Chevron bucks he'd arranged for Marsden's release. The warden agreed, but a judge would have to stamp the decree. Come back tomorrow. Next day Larry appeared, but the warden had disappeared. His replacement announced that Marsden had been executed by firing squad.

Larry's tone, I thought, was jingoistic and presumptive, and beneath the Hail Fellow Well Met I suspected he was capable of being ruthless. I was hurting, and I wanted justice.

"You pushed Marsden to go north," I said. "That night before the break-in."

"That grain was his. He needed it to fill the gaps here."

"You knew there'd be a gap. You planned to produce it that very night. Why, Larry? You're not making enough off the oil franchise? Drumming up some grain running on the side?"

"Slow down, girl," he said. "Nobody got hurt that night. Why the screws?"

"One man kidnapped by SPLA, then later exploded! And another one executed! And don't call me 'girl.'"

Larry turned to Beryl. "Can you talk some sense into your pal?"

"I'm just the court recorder here, tapping away," Beryl said.

He set down his glass. "I'm an oil man. I sign a contract; I fulfill that contract. Case closed. No way do I meddle in politics!"

"You're saying that bribing a warden isn't politics?" Beryl said.

"To do business you've got to have pals." He leaned in. "Ladies, compared to an oil contract, grain is tiddlywinks. Why would I bother?"

The image of Marsden's shirt of fishes hovered in the air.

"The government made it lucrative for you to bother," I said. "Help us get Marsden in a compromising position so we can arrest him and close down his operation. Then we can starve out these southern nigs without nosy, interfering internationals watching. You've heard the word 'genocide'? You stole food from nursing mothers, Larry. Did you get a fat check? From funds supplied the Khartoum honchos by your very own government?"

"You're hurting," Larry said. "You lost a good man."

"Make that two," I said.

"Larry," Beryl said, "in my book you're Number One." She filled his glass. "I'm not pressing charges, I swear. Just give us the nookie."

"Way I heard it," he said, "was the brigadier had a trader pal who set up the train deal. This trader's on the brigadier's payroll, and he offers to escort the army's ammo shipment. Train comes; they tie on the grain cars, head south. SPLA's a wild card. When they show up, the trader and his pals melt into the night. Marsden's spared, but by the time he gets to Wau, Khartoum is hopping mad. Biggest pot of gold they'd shipped, and now the rebels take it. So first they read this brigadier the riot act. Now this brigadier gets hopping mad. Way I figure it he decides to save his ass by implicating Marsden. Tells Khartoum that it sure looks like that UN man was in with the rebels—guy masquerading as aid worker while oiling the rebels' wheels. So this brigadier tells Khartoum he did not give Marsden permission to join that train." Larry leaned forward. "Presto: brigadier's reinstated, and Khartoum gets on the horn to Wau and tells General Adide to arrest Hargreave. Now everybody's happy. Brigadier gets Khartoum off his back, and Khartoum just may get the UN out of the south—because if they off Marsden, chances are the UN will pull out in a huff." He paused. "Though then they risk the threat of sanctions. But we need their oil, so probably sanctions will go on hold."

Larry emptied his glass and leaned back. He was pleased with his performance.

"And the break-in here?" I said.

"Khartoum's of the opinion it was SPLA."

Beryl's voice was even. "Are you saying that you did not set Marsden up and that you had nothing to do with the break-in?"

"Lady, I'm your countryman. Give me credit for your basic decency. Wasn't I raised under the Stars and Stripes just like you? You've heard of liberty and justice for all?"

"Under the Stars and Stripes," Beryl said, "there's always a gun rack in the next room. A man like you with a head for business knows that. So come clean. Educate us. We're a couple of women on our knees in the dirt filling bowls for skeletons. You can trust us."

"You're a couple of handsome dames with pistols in your pocketbooks. Didn't I already get the water torture and the hanging upside down and the cattle prod?"

I tried to imagine in Larry the sudden presence of compunction. I pictured him in the sandbox banging a frilly playmate on the head with a plastic shovel. His mother kneels. "Larrykins, honeybunch, what did Mommy tell you? Do unto others!" In the brain's massive archive had that phrase perchance got shelved? Might some minion of the synapses occasionally nudge the volume from its niche, open it to the light? I was running full out, courtesy of Chevron Scotch, heading for the intersection, no brakes.

"You just happened to be here that particular night?" I said.

"You've heard of this thing random chance?" Larry said.

"Men under the Stars and Stripes have backup," Beryl said. "Who's the backup?"

Larry laughed. "I give up. Write the confession. I'll sign anything."

"Maybe someone set you up," I said. "Told you if you didn't help out, he wouldn't renew your contract. There you were, back to the wall."

Larry was, Beryl would say later, un-fucking-believable.

"Who set you up?" Beryl said. "Anyone we might be acquainted with?"

Larry grinned. "No one you ladies know."

They don't let anyone near the oil fields now. If once there were trees, they've been cleared. The only visitors are lorry drivers hauling supplies. For this reason an old Dinka woman sets up her tea business beside the dirt track. She arrives before dawn and unrolls a mat, sets up the small stove, the kettle, cups. A Kenyan guard from the compound brings her water in exchange for tea. If not for him, she'd have to carry it, and she's too old.

In the south an old Latuka woman polishes John Garang's boots. In the north a Dinka woman serves President Bashir tea. There will always be women stripping leaves from trees, women in cities scavenging from dumpsters. And there will be mines. "To get rid of a foot," Garang had said, "a blast mine's the answer. But should you wish to drink the hemlock, what you want is a frag mine. Best of all's the bounding frag mine. It leaps up to the level of the heart, then bang. Anyone within half a mile comes along for the ride."

There was a market for Valsella's bounding frag mine called the Valmara 69, and there were docile workers in Castenedolo, Italy. A job is a job, and you do what's required—nature of the beast, and the beast owns you. Except Franca Faita, who got together with two girlfriends one June evening over a glass of Chianti. You have to see this video, Franca said. So there in the scented evening the three watched footage in which one child after another steps on a frag mine and disappears.

So lit were these three by passion that they became like medieval saints. With the outrage that translates to courage they convinced the union to demonstrate against Valsella. Franca Faita's banner read: Why do we have to kill to work? Her banner swept the mayor off his feet, and there came a groundswell against Valsella. Valsella's profits had attracted Fiat, and so Valsella gave up the manufacture of mines and took up the manufacture of Fiats. Though before the switch, the executives sold the mine inventory to a German supplier, who in turn sold it in parcels to a number of African governments. In this way a great number of Valmara 69s came into southern Sudan.

———

The immortals can be nudged, Garang had said. I imagine him walking London twilight, brought into the flow of people on the street as though he belonged—until a passerby hurled the word "nig," the gestalt flipped, and he was cast out, watching the flow go past him. I remember his voice. "Queen Victoria's right hand man, General Gordon, comes to Africa to take down the slave trade, and who does he hire as his guide? That notorious slaver Abu Saoud! Backhanders!"

There was that moment when I lowered the binoculars and watched the dust settling. I imagined the angels and archangels of SAR11, that chorus swimming along. I imagined the blue wind weaving, the air giving itself to me to breathe. Heat, that lover, put its mouth everywhere on me. Did I hear the whistling thorn tree, where the wind rushed across the ant holes in its galls? Did I note in the distance the baobab, which given world enough will live two thousand years?

That sound coming from me—sound not mine and yet mine—wound me in its linen, and I thought of the fishy Christ shirt. If I walked to that place, might I find a bit of blue or yellow to hold in my hand?

Or if I sifted the dirt, my mother's ring?

A ring? A bit of cloth? Are you crazy?

The image of Monyluak rose—my monk, hands clasped, weeping, and I imagined myself with a *kwol-jok*, tossing the halves of that cuke up into the air until I got the result I wanted. Annie, sweet girl, the mother in me whispered, this the gods don't take back.

That was when I bowed down in the dirt road. Annie, I told myself, you are going to have to learn to lose.

If we had been given a whole life together, would we have evolved into fat cats, juggling guilt and aspiration over dusky glasses of Merlot? Felicia would have loved him, and our father put on a showy bash—relieved I hadn't chosen a home boy. He'd have stressed the Cambridge bit and joked about his son-in-law taking tea with the queen. But there were still neighborhoods where a black couldn't buy a house or paid too much and later a window was smashed. We'd have walked, he and I, beneath the gaze of curious and sometimes disapproving strangers. And when he walked alone? Or if a cop pulled him over? "I'll do what Kofi did," Garang had said, "when he was a student in the U.S. Kofi's traveling around the country, and one of your southern barbers tells him no haircuts for nigs. Kofi says, I'm not a nig. I'm an African. Well then, says this barber, come on in."

There is innocence in not knowing too much about the lover. Two bodies grapple tenderly inside their spun cocoon of trust, each with their imagined image of the other, and then they take each other's hand and step off the cliff. There, in free fall, they set up house, eat air, drink dew. They begin to tell each other their stories, but these stories are runes to be deciphered by time. What I knew was that Garang had chosen me, and I'd chosen him. Beyond that we'd been two children teetering inside twilight, needing each other and SAR11 to go on.

"Hold me in the fire," Rumi says, "and though I die, I know for whom and why." We fasten on one person, the lover, because we think the lover is the love. But the lover is doing temp work, on loan from the stacked grain bags of the universe. You can steal and steal from this warehouse, and it's OK because the warehouse is perpetually full.

The last night in camp I stood beneath the splash of stars. The dark around them seemed to seethe with fullness. I felt the life of that place burning, the dark buzzing like low fire. Garang wasn't there, but he'd been there, and the place bore his print. Now his absence was part of the rising and multiplying that's always going on. He was there in the mass of dark offering itself, kissing my shoulder, and those kisses felt like a thunderous chorus. Garang, I thought, had kissed my shoulder many times, and now here he was again, still kissing.

What I have now is the Levi's. When everyone's asleep in their tent, I take them out and feel the tight weave of denim. Imagine me in those moments. I'm like St. Teresa, progressing through her beads. And now when I fill a skeleton's bowl, I say to myself, This one's for you, Garang. And this one. And this one. This one's for you.

I was his Tamarisk. Now I know how the saints live. They love; they lose; they go on loving. There isn't any end to love, nor is there an end to feeding and being fed. And I tell you this: even where there's no food, the saints are happy because they are always eating. They eat the looking of all those eyes that meet theirs. They eat the sky and swaying trees; they drink the waters of great rivers. And they eat the soil into which they will die. They look at each other and laugh at each other and themselves and eat the laughing air.

VII

There is no conflict.

This is not a story about evil.

Gringos aren't the bad guys, not exactly. Nor are we innocent.

Garang used to imitate and make fun of the northern Arab's mind-set: Get that black scum off the land—we olive skins need acreage. But in regard to these northerners we have both irony to indulge and amends to make. In Khartoum taxis honk, donkeys bleat, there is dust, and on the periphery the refugee camp houses a million southerners, and how is General-Turned-President

Bashir to feed them when he's broke—if it weren't for the Nuer's oil?

Northerners have needs like anyone else.

Khartoum needs the water of both Niles and no more sandstorms.

Khartoum needs bubble bath and instant messaging and smuggling rhino horns and ivory to the Far East.

Khartoum needs solar power panels and a woman president.

Khartoum needs the waterless urinal and *A Course in Miracles* and condoms and antidepressants and Golfers Anonymous, and they already have their version of that addictive, corporate handheld Blackberry called the Crackberry.

Khartoum needs the al-Morgan development's hotels, banks, and forty thousand jobs, and Khartoum needs the runways extended and maintained so container shipments can come in. Anything you want, it's at the container warehouse. You need a frig? Medicines? Brazilian beer? A 4 x 4 jeep? American cigs? Some tomatoes? Sting CDs?

Khartoum needs to sell licenses illegally and to falsify records and to fabricate evidence and to counterfeit bank notes, credit cards, and IDs and to traffic in radioactive material, human organs, ball bearings, and software.

Khartoum needs to fuck up like every other government except Costa Rica. Khartoum needs to escape reality and to get real.

You think you're better than Khartoum? You want Khartoum to go on its knees and lick your polished toenails and take you all expenses paid to Tahiti and then to shut up?

And Khartoum needs to feel consulted. It's time to listen to Khartoum. Your enemy is your only hope. Are you listening? Do not write Khartoum off! Khartoum is not your own personal punching bag for taking out aggression in the basement.

Khartoum is tired of being the bad guy, so let's give Khartoum a break.

There are those in Khartoum who oppose the government's policies, and now, after years of opposition in exile, the Democratic Unionist Party reopened its office in Khartoum on Friday. Khartoum needs to shake hands with the leader of the DUP, and then Khartoum needs a seat at the table and to break some good bread with the West, and I don't mean a pack of halal MRE rations made 100 percent in America, including New York–style bagel chips in a bag depicting the Big Apple's skyline and Kellogg's Froot Loops (so bad that Saddam in prison tried to trade them for Kellogg's Raisin Bran).

Only Khartoum can free you from fear and show you who you are and what you stand for and whisper in your ear, Remember, one day you will die.

Let's offer Khartoum librarians and string theory and a Michael Franti and Spearhead concert in the Square and the country's dignity recognized.

And later that evening, a drug of Khartoum's choice.

Khartoum needs to be able to rest on its laurels and to rest from its labors and to rest easy and to submit to God five times a day and to rest for the night in an upscale stucco villa on a quiet side street far from the center of the city.

Khartoum needs a vacation. Then it needs another vacation. It needs guaranteed paid vacation leave just like you.

And Khartoum needs to rest assured that even if it loses all its money, you will arrive like God in a limo, and it will be taken care of.

Then some belly dancers serving sorbet would be nice.

No conflict frees us both. You can pick up a bus schedule, drop your SUV keys in the trash, and go to work at Planned Parenthood. People everywhere are nicer when they have fewer children. I'll harangue the populace about condoms. A lot more condoms could change the world, and remember that an injury to a student in Prague strikes down simultaneously a worker in Nairobi, and the minute hand on the doomsday clock has moved forward again—

And then there's me, yours truly—and what am I doing to upgrade our circumstances? So far the Great Mother and Father in the sky have not pushed my face in the dirt and said, "Clean up your act," but they will. Meanwhile I'm dancing as fast as I can in the other direction. And just today I paid my $99 annual carbon offset to Carbonfund—which uses the dollars to buy carbon credits from big-time polluters and then does not resell these credits but retires them so that no other polluter can use them.

But there's more to be done, and quickly! I face the mirror and ask: Am I working to get African debt canceled? Have I striven even a little bit for prison reform? Have I educated myself and my neighbors about alternative fuels? I confess: I mostly lounge in self-satisfied pajamas, blabbering, and let others walk the walk.

Why am I not right this minute writing a check to Concern? Don't I know a kid starves to death every seven seconds? Everybody wants to go on eating, even on the last day, and those lorries keep not arriving, and in the photo Hidaya Abatemam is six years old and weighs seventeen pounds. Her face puzzled. Am I so bad a girl that no one will feed me? Her face is also scared. And betrayed. And anguished. These words lie flat on the page. These words are not the photo of her face, the photo of her face is not her actual face, and I am not where she is.

Get on this now, Big Talker!

Marilyn Krysl

has published three collections of stories, six volumes of poetry, and her work has appeared in *The Atlantic, The Nation, The New Republic, The Pushcart Prize Anthology, Best American Short Stories, O. Henry Prize Stories, Sudden Fiction,* and *Sudden Stories.* She is the recipient of two NEA fellowships, and has taught ESL in the Peoples' Republic of China, served as Artist in Residence at the Center for Human Caring, and worked for Peace Brigade International in Sri Lanka and at the Kalighat Home for the Destitute and Dying, administered by Mother Teresa's Sisters of Charity in Calcutta. She volunteers in Boulder with the Lost Boys of Sudan and helped found C-SAW, the community of Sudanese and American Women, which strives to provide education for Sudanese refugees.